D0097613

BREAKING UP

by the same author

fiction

MY LIFE CLOSED TWICE
JACK BE NIMBLE
STAR TURN
WITCHCRAFT

plays

MY BROTHER'S KEEPER
COUNTRY DANCING

BREAKING UP

NIGEL WILLIAMS

faber and faber
LONDON · BOSTON

First published in 1988
by Faber and Faber Limited
3 Queen Square London WC1N 3AU

Typeset by Wilmaset, Birkenhead, Wirral
Printed in Great Britain by
Mackays of Chatham Ltd, Kent
All rights reserved

© Nigel Williams, 1988

This book is sold subject to the condition that it shall not,
by way of trade or otherwise, be lent, resold, hired out
or otherwise circulated without the publisher's prior consent
in any form of binding or cover other than that in which
it is published and without a similar condition including this
condition being imposed on the subsequent purchaser.

British Library Cataloguing in Publication Data

Williams, Nigel
Breaking up.
I. Title
822'.914   PR6073.I4327
ISBN 0-571-15121-3

To Judy

Breaking Up was first transmitted on BBC2 between 19 November and 10 December 1986 in four episodes. The cast included:

MRS MAILER	Eileen Atkins
MR MAILER	Dave King
JOHN MAILER	Jerome Flynn
TONY MAILER	Tim Haynes
MR JACKSON	John Fortune
MRS JACKSON	Wendy Allnutt
JACKSON	Alex Crockatt
MR POSNER	Alan Bennett
TERRY	Nita Gavin
MARCIA	Rosemary Martin
CLARE	Gabrielle Lloyd
WIGGINS	Roy Heather
TOMKINSON	David Lloyd Meredith
OFF LICENCE OWNER	Danny Schiller
HORVATCH	George Ganchev
Director	Stuart Burge
Producer	Sally Head
Designer	Dick Coles
Script Editor	Gwenda Bagshaw
Editor	Tariq Anwar
Costume designer	Robin Stubbs

EPISODE ONE

Day 1. Monday, 7 October 1985

1. INT. SCHOOL. DAY

A classroom in a public school in North London. It is shortly after the beginning of the Michaelmas term. HUGHES, WANAMAKER, *and* JACKSON, *three boys of thirteen or fourteen, are singing 'Diamond Ring Blues' by Sunny Terry and Brawne McGee.* JACKSON *is a handsome youth, rather well dressed;* HUGHES *is one of those preternaturally hairy boys, with a somewhat Mexican look about him, while* WANAMAKER *is . . . well, since* WANAMAKER *does not figure much in this story, there is little point in describing him. Boys singing 'Hoochie Coochie Song'.* TONY MAILER *comes in from the corridor. A studious-looking boy who has the disadvantage of looking young for his age.*

MAILER: I shouldn't make too much noise.

JACKSON: Why not?

MAILER: Loopy's on the war path.

JACKSON: Come on, Mailer. Verse two.
   (*All the lads are doing mimed harmonies, blues stuff.*)

MAILER: OK. (*A pause.*) I need a ruler and a rubber. (*Pause.*) One, two, three. (*Picking up his briefcase and leaving*) I don't feel like it.

WANAMAKER: You OK?

MAILER: I'm all right. Come on, Jackson.

2. INT. TUBE. DAY

The tube rattling overland through the suburbs. No one else in the compartment. MAILER *and* JACKSON *are seated next to each other sharing a bag of crisps.*

MAILER: Jackson –

JACKSON: Yes?

MAILER: Do your parents get on?

JACKSON: It's disgusting.

MAILER: How do you mean?

JACKSON: Oh, they kiss. When he comes in from chambers. (*Pause.*) A great, slobbery, wet kiss.

MAILER: I think that's nice.

JACKSON: It's nice for them I suppose. (*Pause.*) I think it's disgusting.

MAILER: I've never seen my parents kiss.

JACKSON: Perhaps they do it when you're not looking.

3. INT. MAILER'S HOUSE. DAY

We see MAILER *coming in to the back door of his parents' suburban home. When he gets into the kitchen, a large room, he stops. Listens. He can hear a distant adult argument. Loud voices.*

MRS MAILER: (*Out of vision*) All I don't know is why I was so stupid as not to see it, my god, everyone else must have been able to, they must have been amusing themselves at my expense, I . . .

MR MAILER: (*Out of vision*) No one else knew.

MRS MAILER: (*Out of vision*) No one else, everyone knew. Did you have a special pub you went to?

MR MAILER: (*Out of vision*) I . . . I just thought . . .

MRS MAILER: (*Out of vision*) And why now? Why do you have to tell me now? Now rather than any other time in the last seven years? I just don't see why.

(*As* MAILER*'s listening his elder brother* JOHN, *a large good-looking young man in his early twenties, comes in behind him.* JOHN *is far less posh-sounding than his younger brother, perhaps because he didn't go to a public school, but we should see instantly that these two are very fond of each other.*)

JOHN: Hiya, genius.

MAILER: I wouldn't go through there.

MR MAILER: (*Out of vision*) Because I was fed up with it, that's why, I was fed up with making excuses.

MRS MAILER: (*Out of vision*) Excuses for what?

MR MAILER: (*Out of vision*) You know, excuses. The way you make excuses the whole time. Christ, it hasn't been exactly fun having you around looking about as interested as a . . .

MRS MAILER: (*Out of vision*) Well, you didn't try hard to make me feel any better.

(JOHN *goes into the hall and listens.*)

2

JOHN: God. (*Sits.*) Why don't they go to work like other
    parents?
MAILER: He's always here at the moment.
    (*The row continues.*)
MRS MAILER: (*Pause, out of vision*) Did you talk about me
    then? Did you, you and her, 'The wife is a bit . . .'
MR MAILER: (*Out of vision*) I never talked about you like that, I
    swear I didn't. I never did talk about you like that.
MRS MAILER: (*Out of vision*) How do you expect me to believe
    that? How do you expect me to trust you ever again?
MR MAILER: (*Out of vision*) I don't.
    (*Pause.*)
MRS MAILER: (*Out of vision*) What do you want to do now?
MR MAILER: (*Out of vision*) What do you mean, 'do now'?
MRS MAILER: (*Out of vision*) Now, what do you want to do
    now? You are going to have to do something, aren't you?
JOHN: Well, he's going bloody broke, isn't he? I don't know.
    (*Pause.*) Is there any tea?
MAILER: I suppose she'll do it. Eventually.
    (*And he is going to the door.*)
JOHN: Where are you off to?
MAILER: I've got Greek prep.
JOHN: (*Shouting after him*) You'll strain your eyes!

4. INT. MAILER'S HOUSE. DAY
Hall and stairs. We see MAILER *go out into the hall and head for
the stairs. He stops outside the drawing room and the voices inside
are suddenly lowered. He sets out for the stairs. When he's halfway
up, his mother, a taut-looking woman in her fifties, comes out. She is
in tears.* MAILER *watches impassively. She doesn't see him. Then,
just as he is about to go on up, his father, a thickset man, with a
strong, one might almost say passionate, physical presence, emerges.
He looks up and sees his son. Like his eldest son,* MR MAILER *has a
strong London accent.*
MR MAILER: Hullo, mate.
MAILER: Hullo, Dad.
MR MAILER: You got homework then?

3

MAILER: Greek.

MR MAILER: Bloody good, mate. Bloody good. (*Going to the stairs; a warm smile*) I wish I'd've had Greek when I was at school, I tell you.

MAILER: Yeah?

MR MAILER: Greek would'a bin bloody useful to me.

MAILER: Do you think so?

MR MAILER: Extremely so?

(MAILER *sits, his formal manner contrasting oddly with his father's*.)

MAILER: I don't see what use Greek would have been in the haulage business.

MR MAILER: I wouldn't'a *bin* in the haulage business, would I?

MAILER: Oh.

MR MAILER: I'd have bin in the Greek business.

MAILER: I must do my prose.

MR MAILER: Eh, come here. Give us a hug.

(*He goes to him and puts his arm round him. He kisses him.*)

5. INT. MAILER'S HOUSE. EVENING

MAILER *in his bedroom working. It is not conventionally what you might expect of a boy's room. Instead of pictures of athletic heroes or pop stars, there are several large colour photos of what look like Greek temples, and a large number of books.* JOHN *comes in and throws himself on the bed.* MAILER *carries on working.*

JOHN: He's pissed again.

MAILER: I know.

JOHN: Disgusting old bastard.

MAILER: Mmmm. (*Then he puts down his pen.*) Do you really hate him?

JOHN: I wish he was dead.

MAILER: He soon will be if he carries on like this.

JOHN: I'd like to dance on his grave. In hobnailed boots.

MAILER: Yes. (*Pause.*) I quite like him actually. (*Pause.*) It's her that gives me the creeps.

JOHN: Abandon ship, mate. While there's still time.

MAILER: Is that what you're going to do?

4

(JOHN *gets up.*)

JOHN: (*Sensing his little brother's sudden panic*) Not yet, Titch. (*Ruffling his hair*) I'll stand by you.

Day 2. Tuesday, 8 October

6. INT. MAILER'S HOUSE. DAY

Breakfast. MR *and* MRS MAILER *and their younger son in the kitchen.*

MR MAILER: Where's that boy?

MRS MAILER: He's asleep.

MR MAILER: What do you mean asleep – I'll give him frigging sleep . . .

MRS MAILER: He's been working . . .

MR MAILER: I'm up, aren't I? I'm up! There's no reason why he shouldn't be up.

MRS MAILER: Stop it, stop it, stop it.

7. EXT. STREET. DAY

Outside Mailer's house. We see MAILER *walking off down the street. At almost the same moment, obviously a regular routine,* JACKSON *comes out of a house not far now on the other side of the road.* MAILER *crosses to him.*

JACKSON: Hullo, Mailer.

MAILER: Hullo. (*Pause. As they walk on*) They're killing each other in there.

JACKSON: Yeah?

MAILER: I wish they'd get a divorce or something.

JACKSON: Really?

MAILER: Really.

(JACKSON *finds this very puzzling.*)

You know what people say about staying together because of the children?

JACKSON: Yes.

MAILER: It's rubbish.

5

8. INT. SCHOOL. DAY

*Lunchtime. The stage of the main hall, known locally as 'Big
School'. A lot of wood and shields and, out front, an empty waste of
chairs.* MAILER *is with* MR POSNER, *a dramatic and kindly sort of
schoolmaster, who is also his housemaster.* MAILER *is reading from
a Penguin classic.*

PATTERSON: 'To a nunnery, go.'

MAILER: 'O, what a noble mind is here o'erthrown!
    The courtier's, soldier's, scholar's, eye, tongue, sword,
    Th' expectancy and rose of the fair state,
    The glass of fashion and the mould of form,
    Th' observ'd of all observers, quite, quite down!
    And I, of ladies most deject and wretched – '
    (MR POSNER *leaps in, gesturing enthusiastically.*)

POSNER: 'And I, of ladies most deject and wretched . . .'

MAILER: Yes, sir.

POSNER: Let the words dance on your tongue, Mailer. You're a
    high-born Elizabethan lady.

MAILER: I know, sir.

POSNER: Patterson confuses you. Sometimes he seems to love
    you – sometimes he's talking wildly about your chastity.

MAILER: Yes, sir.
    (*From the back of the stage we see* PATTERSON, *a large,
    handsome sixth-former who is also Mailer's house captain.
    There is a rugged naïveté about him that makes him entirely
    unsuitable for the role of Hamlet.*)

PATTERSON: May I go, sir? I've got fives.

POSNER: Of course, Patterson. Tomorrow, at the lunch hour.

PATTERSON: Yes, sir. (*As he is going*) I've got cross-country at
    twelve thirty, sir. Thank you, sir.
    (PATTERSON *goes.*)

POSNER: I think we may have miscast Patterson, Mailer.

MAILER: Do you, sir?

POSNER: Does he strike you as quite up to Hamlet?

MAILER: I don't know, sir. (*Pause.*) I'm not sure I'm up to
    Ophelia.

POSNER: I think you would be a more suitable Hamlet, Mailer?

MAILER: Really, sir?

POSNER: You reek of existential gloom.

MAILER: Patterson's awfully good-looking, sir.

POSNER: I cast on the face. Never cast on the face. Cast on the
inner light. (*Watching* MAILER *shrewdly*) Are you all right,
boy?

MAILER: Yes, sir.
(*The master crosses to him.*)

POSNER: Your tie's at half-mast, boy.

MAILER: Sorry, sir.

POSNER: How's your da?

MAILER: Fine.

POSNER: Does he still go to the Feathers?

MAILER: I think so, sir.

POSNER: Maybe I'll pop in one night. He's all right?

MAILER: He's fine, sir.

POSNER: Times are hard in the haulage business. (*Ruffling his
hair*) So long Ophelia.
(*And he goes.*)

9. INT. MAILER'S HOUSE. DAY

*Stairs and hall. Mrs Mailer's bedroom. There are big pictures of
John everywhere. John at school. John in a football team. John
with his mates. One of Tony. MRS MAILER is standing at the door
of their bedroom watching her husband. She has what is going to be
quite a nasty bruise on her lip. MR MAILER is going through his
things roughly and packing what he needs into a case. When he's
finished with the clothes, he picks up a picture of Tony on the desk.*

MR MAILER: Shall I take this?

MRS MAILER: Take what you want. You can't come back, if
you're going to her I won't have you back. I won't have
you back if you go to bloody Marcia now. Don't think you
will ever get back here ever, ever.

MR MAILER: Look . . .

MRS MAILER: Got all you need?

MR MAILER: I don't know what I need.

10. INT. SCHOOL. DAY

When POSNER's *gone* MAILER *struts about.*

MAILER: (*Suddenly forceful*) '. . . the beauty of the world, the paragon of animals – and yet, to me, what is this quintessence of dust? Man delights not me – nor woman neither, though – '

(JACKSON *has come in and is standing at the back of the hall.*)

JACKSON: You're jolly good.

MAILER: You should have said you were there.

JACKSON: I was listening. You are good.

MAILER: I'm no good when anyone's listening.

JACKSON: I thought acting was showing off.

MAILER: It's being someone else I like.

(*He jumps down into the hall and the two boys go out through the waste of empty chairs.*)

I mean I don't like being a girl much. But it's better than being me.

11. INT. MAILER'S HOUSE. DAY

MRS MAILER: How does she do it then? Does she do it the way you like it, does she put on a big performance, does she?

MR MAILER: I'm sorry, I didn't want it to be this way.

MRS MAILER: Well, it's the way you are going to get it.

(MR MAILER *is now in the hall. He puts down the case and she comes after him.*)

Did you take the boy to see her? Does he know her?

MR MAILER: Mary . . .

MRS MAILER: Were you going to drop off at the school and pick him up as well, was that it? You want everything, don't you?

MR MAILER: For God's sake, Mary.

(*She pushes past him, heading for the telephone, dials furiously.*)

For God's sake.

MRS MAILER: (*Dialling*) Oh no, you don't. (*Into telephone*) Hello, it's Mrs Mailer, Tony Mailer, 4A, can you get a message to him, please . . . ? It's just that I need him at

home very urgently . . . yes . . . yes, there's been an
accident, I need him very urgently at home. Could you get
that message to him, please?
(*She puts the telephone down.*)

MR MAILER: What the hell are you doing?

MRS MAILER: And then he can see just how wonderful his dad
really is, can't he? It's you leaving us, remember that.
You're leaving us, not the other way round. (*Pause, colder*)
Because you turn him against me all the time. All the time
you turn him against me, don't you?

12. INT. SCHOOL. DAY

JACKSON *and* MAILER *going down the steps to the entrance hall.*

JACKSON: Well.

MAILER: Would you mind coming with me, Jackson?

JACKSON: How do you mean?

MAILER: He says there's been an accident. I'll cover for you.
(*Pause.*) It's only Art. Matthews won't notice.

JACKSON: Do you think it's a bad accident?

MAILER: There's no such thing as an accident in our house. It's
all done deliberately.

JACKSON: Oh. (*Slightly puzzled by this in the way he sometimes is
by* MAILER.) All right.

13. INT. MAILER'S HOUSE. DAY

*The cubby hole that does as Mr Mailer's office. He's getting the
books and papers he might need. There's far too much to take and,
anyway, he was not ready to leave this quickly. He stops, picks up a
book, dithers, another of the cash books. What is he to do?* MRS
MAILER *picks up stuff and chucks it at him. He takes what few
books he can and makes his way down the hall where he has left his
suitcase.*

MR MAILER: I will come back for the stuff I need.

MRS MAILER: Are you going straight to her? Is that where
you're going?

MR MAILER: If you don't want me to go, I won't.
(MR MAILER *picks up the case.*)

MRS MAILER: How often apart from the time in Manchester, and when you went to the exhibition? How often?

MR MAILER: Why do you have to know?

MRS MAILER: And weekends. You said weekends. How many weekends? Every weekend?

MR MAILER: Listen, Mary, what I feel for her is . . .

MRS MAILER: It's obvious what you feel for her, isn't it? (*Violent almost obscene sexual gesture, showing the suppressed sexuality of the woman.*) This, this, this, this, isn't it? (*He's at the door by now. She goes to the drinks cabinet in the front room and begins to pull out the bottles.*)

14. EXT. STREET. DAY

Coming up to Mailer's house. JACKSON *and* MAILER *stop some way away. Mailer's mum and dad are in the middle of an argument that has erupted into the street.*

MRS MAILER: Well, go to her then and see how you like it. If that's what you want, you go to her.

MR MAILER: I'm going. I'm going. (*She's throwing clothes, cases, and other things she thinks of as his out into the street. All her usual carefully controlled gentility gone.*)

MRS MAILER: And get your drink out of it an' all, all you ever bring is debts, debts, debts.

MR MAILER: For Christ's sake, get off my back, will you.

MRS MAILER: Let her keep you, get out of it, you hear me, out of it. (*She's hurling stuff straight at* MR MAILER. MAILER *and* JACKSON *watching.*)

JACKSON: Blimey . . .

MAILER: I knew that would be it.

JACKSON: Are they drunk?

MAILER: Probably. (*His dad is coming down the street towards them.*)

MRS MAILER: *And don't come crawling back, OK? Don't think you can come crawling back!* I don't want to see your face again, now get out.

10

MR MAILER: Don't worry, I won't . . .
  (*And he sees* MAILER *and* JACKSON.)
  Oh. (*Pause.*) Hullo there.
MAILER: Hullo, Dad.
MR MAILER: What are you doing here?
MAILER: She rang the school.
MR MAILER: Oh yeah –
MAILER: I was told to come home.
MR MAILER: I'm sorry, boy. (*Sits on the pavement, near to tears.*)
  She loves it. You know that? She likes you to 'ave a
  ringside seat.
JACKSON: Look, I think I better go.
MAILER: Please don't just yet, I –
MR MAILER: This is your mate, isn't it?
MAILER: You know Jackson, Dad.
MR MAILER: Oh yes. (*Pause.*) I know Jackson. (*Pause.*) Look,
  I'll be back, OK? I won't be long, OK? (*Pulls himself
  together enough to realize that one of his son's friends is there.*)
  Look. I've got . . . (*Pause.*) You know . . .
  (*And somehow or other he gets himself to his feet and walks
  off.*)
JACKSON: Are you going in?
MAILER: Do you mind if I go into your house for a bit?
JACKSON: No. Not at all. I'd have to ask. (*But not quite at ease
  with his sudden dependence*) Would you go and live with him?
MAILER: I don't want to live with any of them. I'd rather live in
  a tent. Frankly.
JACKSON: I know what you mean.
MAILER: Oh your family's all right. Yours is great really.
JACKSON: You wouldn't say that if you had to live there.
  (*They are crossing the road to Jackson's house. We can see* MR
  JACKSON, *a florid man of theatrical appearance, through the
  window.* JACKSON *looks at him darkly.*)
  Just look at him.
  (*And* MR JACKSON, *who is in fact a barrister by trade, has
  seen the boys and opens the door to them with the kind of
  flourish that suggests he is a very ham performer.*)

II

MR JACKSON: Welcome, sweet boys.

JACKSON: Can Mailer come to tea?

MR JACKSON: Can Mailer come to tea? Does the earth go round the sun? Do stars have fires? *Do* the little birds open their beaks to wake us at an unseasonable hour? Are yams an exotic vegetable?

(MRS JACKSON *appears behind* MR JACKSON. *A motherly woman well able to cope with her husband.*)

MRS JACKSON: Of course you can, Mailer. You're always welcome.

15. INT. JACKSON'S HOUSE. NIGHT

The living room, cosy. MR JACKSON *is at the curtains, hamming as usual.*

MR JACKSON: All is quiet. No sound disturbs the hearth. A light burns in the window. Calling you.

MRS JACKSON: Would you like some more carrot cake?

MAILER: No thanks, Mrs Jackson. It was lovely. (*Realizes he is overstaying his welcome.*) I really ought to go, I suppose.

MRS JACKSON: I'm afraid you ought.

MR JACKSON: You will make a charming Ophelia. (*Strikes a pose.*)

'Anon he find him,
Striking too short at Greeks. His antique sword,
Rebellious to his arm, lies where it falls,
Repugnant to command – '

(*Trying to cheer* MAILER *up by clowning*) People found my Player King a little overstated. 'Take it down,' they kept saying. 'Take it down.' 'I can't,' I said. 'I'm up up up.' I said, 'I'm a very up actor.'

MAILER: Were you an actor, Mr Jackson?

MR JACKSON: I was the flower of the Oxford Union. Dramatic Society. I was the jewel in their crown.

JACKSON: Shut up, Dad.

MR JACKSON: You hear the boy? You hear the insolence of the boy?

(*He is actually delighted at everything his son does.*)

MAILER: Thank you, Mr Jackson, thank you, Mrs Jackson.
MRS JACKSON: Look if you're not –
MAILER: I'm all right, Mrs Jackson.
MR JACKSON: Show your guest out, Dumb Insolence.

16. EXT./INT. MAILER'S HOUSE. NIGHT
MAILER *at his front door.*
MRS MAILER: Where've you been? It's evening now.
MAILER: Out.
MRS MAILER: What does 'out' mean? Where out? Out where? I
    rang the school.
MAILER: I was at Jackson's.
MRS MAILER: Why didn't you ring?
MAILER: I just – what happened?
    (*Suddenly her bitterness and anger gets the better of her and she
    pulls the boy roughly into the house.*)
MRS MAILER: Bed.
MAILER: Leave me alone.
MRS MAILER: Upstairs. Now. Bed. You hear?
MAILER: I've got prep.
MRS MAILER: 'Prep'? 'Prep'? What is this performance?
MAILER: Where's Dad? I have to do my prep.
MRS MAILER: You'll do what I say and not what that bloody
    school says. You'll do as *I* say when I say it and that's that
    and I'll bloody well make sure you wipe that smile off of
    your face.
MAILER: Look I just –
MRS MAILER: *Upstairs you! Upstairs you hear?*
    (*She hits the boy. So distraught, she forgets how hard. He
    cowers away terrified but she pursues him.*)
MAILER: *Please don't! Please don't.*
    (*His big brother* JOHN *comes from the kitchen into the hall.*)
JOHN: *Mum!*
    (*She stops.*)
    No, Mum, no. (JOHN *goes to her. The sexual bond between
    these two is very strong.*)
    It isn't down to Tony, Mum, is it? What the old bastard

13

did isn't down to him, is it?

MRS MAILER: Oh John, he's gone. He's gone, he's gone, he's gone.

(*And she weeps as he goes to her.*)

JOHN: Upstairs, Titch. I'll come up.

MRS MAILER: John, don't leave me, don't.

JOHN: Sssh.

MRS MAILER: I can't cope, John, I can't cope, I'm sorry, I just can't take it, I'm sorry.

JOHN: Sssh.

MRS MAILER: John, he's gone, he's gone, I can't . . .

JOHN: Sssh.

(*We see* MAILER *watch all of this from the stairs. Impassive. He turns and goes up to his room.*)

17. INT. MAILER'S HOUSE. NIGHT

MAILER *is sitting up in bed with a Greek textbook.* JOHN *comes in.*

JOHN: Hiya, Titch.

MAILER: Hullo.

JOHN: I brought you a pie.

MAILER: Thanks.

JOHN: No crumbs.

MAILER: Thanks.

(*He wolfs it down.*)

JOHN: What are you doing?

MAILER: Greek.

(JOHN *peers at the book.*)

JOHN: The hoplites took up their stand between the trees. (*Grimace.*) What are hoplites then?

MAILER: Blokes in armour.

JOHN: Oh.

MAILER: They keep taking up their stand. That's all they ever do. Between trees, under mountains, on fields, beside bridges.

(JOHN *grins.*)

Is Dad ever coming back?

JOHN: She says she won't have him back. I don't know. (*Sitting*

on the bed) He's a psychopath.
(MAILER *doesn't react to this.*)
I'd like to upend a loada those insects on to his face. You
know. The ones that eat everything in their way.
MAILER: Termites.
JOHN: 'Come out for a beer, John.' Ugh. He's a warped old
bastard.
MAILER: In Ancient Rome, if you murdered your father they
put you in a bag with a stone and a poisonous snake and
threw you in the Tiber.
JOHN: That sounds about right for him. Maybe we should add a
porcupine. And a rat or two.
MAILER: And her.
JOHN: You're a good kid.
MAILER: Thanks.
JOHN: You're a tough little bugger. Know that? You're a good
kid. (*Getting up*) I'll see you right.
MAILER: Did you sell any fridges today?
JOHN: Yeah. Lots. Keep it up. (*Grins at the door.*) Keep it up.
(*When he's gone*, MAILER *looks at his book. Puts it down.
Close to tears, he stares out at the street.*)

18. INT. MAILER'S HOUSE. NIGHT
The middle of the same night. MAILER *is asleep in bed. There is a
tapping at the window.*
A VOICE: Tony. Tony.
(*We see a shape at the window. Eventually* MAILER *wakes
and looks over. Crosses. It's his father. On a ladder.*)
MAILER: Dad.
MR MAILER: Sssh!
MAILER: Hullo.
MR MAILER: Sssh! (*Pause.*) Where is she?
MAILER: Asleep. (*Still half asleep himself*) Haven't you got your
key?
MR MAILER: The cow Chubb-locked the door, hasn't she?
MAILER: I'll come down.
MR MAILER: Sssh! (*Pause.*) I haven't got long.

MAILER: Aren't you staying?
MR MAILER: Come downstairs and I'll tell you.
  (MAILER *turns*.)
  Quietly.

19. INT. MAILER'S HOUSE. NIGHT
We see MAILER *going out very carefully on to the landing. Checking
his mother's room. Then down the stairs with equal caution. He goes
through to the kitchen and gropes in the dresser for the Chubb key.
Finds it. Stops. Thinks he's heard a noise. Freezes. Goes on out into
the hall. All clear. Very very slowly he crosses to the door and gets
out the key. He has trouble fitting it into the lock but he finally gets
there. He's just about to turn it when he hears a voice behind him.
His mother.*
MRS MAILER: Give that here.
MAILER: It's –
MRS MAILER: Come on. Give it here. (*Pause.*) *Come on!*
MR MAILER: (*Outside*) Tony?
  (*He dare not answer.*)
  Tony, are you there?
MAILER: She's –
  (*But his mother puts her hand over his face.*)
MR MAILER: Tony? You there? Tony?
  (*His mother is pulling him away from the door.*)
  I just want to come in for a second. I need to pick up a
  couple of things. I'm going away but I'll be back. I want
  to –
MRS MAILER: You want to what?
MR MAILER: Mary?
MRS MAILER: I said the door would be locked and I meant it.
  The back door's bolted. Now clear off.
MR MAILER: Mary –
MRS MAILER: I said clear off.
MR MAILER: I wanted to talk to the boy. My things are –
MRS MAILER: I'll send your things on.
MR MAILER: You don't know what you're doing. You –
MRS MAILER: I know just what I'm doing. (*Goes to the door.*)

16

After what you did to my face today I know just what I'm
doing. I'll have a court order on you. The lawyers can send
it to that tart's place.

MR MAILER: Mary –

MRS MAILER: Now clear off.

MR MAILER: Mary! (*Banging on door*) *I wanner talk to the boy!*

MRS MAILER: *Any more of that and I call the law!*

MR MAILER: *I've got my rights!*

MRS MAILER: Oh, you haven't got any rights. After what you
did today you have no rights at all. Now clear off or I
phone the police.

MR MAILER: *Mary!*

(*She and* MAILER *stand in silence. And then they hear his
footsteps retreating.*)

MRS MAILER: That's the last you'll see of *him* . . .

(*She turns to her son for support but terrified and confused he
backs away.*)

Tony, I – (*Frustration turning to anger*) What's up with me?
I got cancer, have I?

(*The boy doesn't speak.*)

What's wrong with me?

MAILER: I hate you. I hate you worse than anyone in the world.
One day when you're not looking I'll kill you. I hope you
die or something. I hope you do get cancer and die. I hate
you. I hate you.

MRS MAILER: Get upstairs.

(*Something about him scares her.*)

Get upstairs!

(*She hits him. He dodges out of her reach and when he's gone
she breaks down. Screaming for her elder son. But he's not
there.*)

Day 3. Wednesday, 9 October

20. INT. MAILER'S HOUSE. EARLY MORNING

Later the same night. MAILER *in bed asleep. Once again a tapping
on the window. Once again it is his father. Wearily he gets up and*

17

staggers over to the window. If there's a funny side to the sight of his dad perched on a ladder, doubtless somewhat drunk, MAILER *is too tired to see it.*

MAILER: I've got to go to school in the morning, Dad.

MR MAILER: I'm sorry, son.

MAILER: I'm knackered.

MR MAILER: I'm sorry, son.

MAILER: She'll hear us. She hears everything.

MR MAILER: I'll be at the Naked Lady. On the North Circ. You know it. Five on Friday. Wait for me there.

MAILER: You what?

MR MAILER: Bring things you want. You know. Any of them books of yours. Anything you specially like.

MAILER: Where are we going then?

MR MAILER: You'll see. We'll be all right. (*Sentimental grin.*) Friday at five. You be there.

MAILER: Can I go to sleep now?

Day 5. Friday, 11 October

21. EXT. SCHOOL. DAY

MAILER *and* JACKSON *in Army Corps uniform going down towards the parade ground.*

MAILER: I'm running away.

JACKSON: Really?
  (*A lot of other boys in Corps uniform are milling around and* JACKSON *and* MAILER *thread their way through them.*)
  Does that mean you'll be leaving school?

MAILER: I don't expect so. I hope not. I'll just have a new address.

JACKSON: What is the British Army today?

MAILER: Tough, disciplined and efficient fighting force.

22. EXT. SCHOOL. DAY

The Parade Ground. MAILER *and* JACKSON *in their platoon.* KITCHEN, *the Sergeant in charge of the platoon, is pacing up and down in front of them. He is a lynx-eyed, fearless second-year sixth-*

former with insane military ambitions. He has a swagger stick.
Not the parade-ground sergeant type. Instead his behaviour seems
to be learned from the low-profile macho of films like The Wild
Geese. *Soft-spoken menace is his speciality.* MAILER *is getting*
to KITCHEN.

KITCHEN: *Quiet, Mailer!* (*Does a bit more of the menace.*) Now
    once again I am about to demonstrate the about turn, quick
    time. Pay attention.
    (*He marches off from the platoon with much dash. You could*
    be forgiven for thinking that he has some firm implement up his
    behind.)

JACKSON: Can you choose which one you go with?

MAILER: I think so. I think they ask you when they get
    divorced.

JACKSON: Are they getting divorced then?

MAILER: I think so. I'm not sure really.

JACKSON: Don't you sue for it or something?

MAILER: Samarkand's parents got divorced. I'll ask him. (*But*
    he looks a little insecure.) I think they let you choose.

KITCHEN: *Mailer, are you listening?*

MAILER: Yes, sir.

KITCHEN: Well, Mailer, if you are listening and have been
    paying attention while I have been demonstrating the about
    turn, quick time, instead of wimping around thinking what
    a wimp you are, Mailer, perhaps you would enjoy stepping
    out in front of the platoon and showing us how.

MAILER: Yes, sir.

KITCHEN: Attention. One pace forward march. Quick march.
    (MAILER *attempts the about turn on the double without a great*
    deal of success.)

23. EXT. SCHOOL. DAY
MAILER *still dressed in his Corps kit with a briefcase full of his*
treasures. He is walking with JACKSON *and* HUGHES *down the hill*
that leads away from the school.

JACKSON: What did you take in the end?

MAILER: The Larousse *World Mythology* and my PVC mac. I

couldn't get anything else in the case.

HUGHES: Are you going somewhere, Mailer?

MAILER: Yes, I'm not going home tonight.

HUGHES: Are you going to a party?

MAILER: I don't really go to parties.

JACKSON: He's going to live with his dad.

HUGHES: Oh.

MAILER: It'll be much better. My mum's a bit . . . (*Taps the side of his head.*) Up here. You know.

HUGHES: It's probably the menopause.

MAILER: The what?

HUGHES: Don't you know about the menopause?

MAILER: Er . . .

(JACKSON *is not giving him any help.*)

Oh, the *menopause.*

HUGHES: Exactly.

24. EXT. STREET. DAY

MAILER *is standing by the 'Naked Lady' (La Délivrance) monument at Temple Fortune. Waiting. Crosses to the kerb. Looks. But doesn't see anything. Goes back to his bench. Pause. Eventually a* MAN *passes.*

MAILER: Excuse me –

MAN: Yeah?

MAILER: Is this the Naked Lady?

MAN: Yeah.

MAILER: Thanks.

MAN: This is it.

(*Pause.*)

MAILER: I'm waiting for someone.

MAN: Ah.

(*Pause. And then he goes.* MAILER *sits. Takes out the mac and the Larousse dictionary. Folds up the mac. It is some time before he puts the things away and, keeping the urge to cry back, walks off alone up the road.*)

25. INT. MAILER'S HOUSE. EVENING

MAILER *coming in from his unsuccessful trip.* JOHN's *there.*

JOHN: Hullo, genius.

MAILER: You've been away.

JOHN: Yeah.

MAILER: Where did you go?

JOHN: A conference. About selling fridges.

MAILER: Was it good?

JOHN: Incredible amounts of crumpet.

MAILER: Oh.

JOHN: Inexhaustible quantities of slippery.

MAILER: That was good then.

JOHN: It was.

MAILER: Where's Dad gone?

JOHN: He's got a bird. Didn't you know?

MAILER: No.

JOHN: They never tell you anything, do they?

MAILER: No.

JOHN: God. Imagine doing it with him. Just imagine it.
Actually *doing* it with Doomburden. (*Pause.*) The mind
boggles.

MAILER: He is coming back, isn't he? Dad.

JOHN: I shouldn't think so. (*Gets up.*) Look, Titch, I've got
something to tell you.

MAILER: What?

JOHN: I've got to go away.

MAILER: Oh. (*Pause.*) Where to?

JOHN: Abroad.

MAILER: Is it to do with fridges? (*Trying not to show how upset
he is*) Or is it slippery?

JOHN: Bit of both, old son. (*Going to him*) I got a job in France,
same company but I have to move. I mean, I have to go
where the work is.

MAILER: I suppose you do.

JOHN: I'll be gone quite a time I'm afraid. Look, I'll talk to her.
I've started to talk to her already. She'll be OK. Now he's
gone she'll be OK.

MAILER: Will she?
JOHN: She'll be fine.
(MRS MAILER *comes in.*)
MRS MAILER: Where were you, Tony?
MAILER: Games.
MRS MAILER: Oh. (*Pause.*) I'll get your tea then.
MAILER: Thanks.
(*She goes.*)
JOHN: See? (*Ruffling his hair*) It's gonna be all *right* . . .

Day 8. Monday, *14 October*

26. INT. MAILER'S HOUSE. DAY
MAILER *is in his room practising his lines.*
MAILER: 'I hope all will be well. We must be patient. But I
cannot choose but weep to think they would lay him i' th'
cold ground. My brother shall know of it. And so I thank
you for your good counsel. Come, my coach – '
(*We hear* MRS MAILER *shouting from the hall – 'Tonee.' At
first* MAILER *does not hear and then the call comes again:
'Tony.' He stops and goes through to the landing. Looks down.
There below in the hall are his mother and* JOHN. JOHN's *with
his cases.*)
Oh.
JOHN: I'm off, Titch.
MAILER: Oh.
JOHN: I'm off, Titch. Back before you know it.
(MAILER *descends the staircase slowly. His brother's easy
charm not making him feel any easier. Mum is near tears.*)
MRS MAILER: Oh, John, I –
JOHN: Ssh, Mum. (*Looking between the two of them*) And you
two try not to tear each other's eyes out, eh? (*To* MAILER)
Be good, genius.
MAILER: Whereabouts in France are you going?
JOHN: Round about the middle.
MRS MAILER: John –

(*She's crying now.* JOHN *puts his arm round her.*)
JOHN: Ssh.
   (MAILER *watches this impassively.*)
   See you later. Remember what I told you, Mum.
   (*And he's gone.*)
MAILER: What did he tell you?
MRS MAILER: Nothing. Nothing.
MAILER: Where's Dad?
MRS MAILER: Don't start. Not now. Don't start.
MAILER: I just wanted to –
MRS MAILER: He's a long way away and he never wants to see
   any of us again, OK? He's never coming back, OK? He's
   disappeared for good, OK? (*Almost as if seeing* TONY *for
   the first time*) Why did we spend all that money on that
   school?
MAILER: I don't know.
MRS MAILER: Schools like that they cause a lot of trouble.
   (*It is true the school uniform is somewhat effortful.*)
MAILER: I've got to practise my lines.
MRS MAILER: Well, don't be practising them too hard, will
   you?
   (*He stops.*)
   (*Almost as if this is the only way she can get through to him.
   By hurting him*) You won't be at that snob's academy much
   longer.
MAILER: Where am I going?
MRS MAILER: Somewhere where they'll knock a bit of sense
   into you. (*Pause.*) I don't know why we thought we had to
   send you there. Not against the law to send you to an
   ordinary school, is it?
MAILER: I don't know.
MRS MAILER: Well, it might do you some good to meet some
   ordinary people. Your mum and dad were bloody ordinary
   enough. Every time I go to that place I felt my face didn't
   fit.
MAILER: Mum.
MRS MAILER: It was all his idea. He's so impressed by things

23

like that. (*Arguing with her husband but addressing the remark to the boy*) Well, I'm not impressed, I'm not.

Day 16. Tuesday, 22 October

27. INT. SCHOOL. DAY
The eve of the dress rehearsal. MAILER *is sitting in a classics lesson, next to* JACKSON. TOMKINSON, *the classics master, is teaching, a bluff sort of fellow.*

TOMKINSON: Virgil wasn't what you'd call a good bloke. In fact in many ways Virgil was a pain in the neck. When people saw Virgil coming I rather expect they said things like 'Oh God, Virgil' and crossed over the road sort of thing. But Virgil was a great poet and this line on the board tells you why.
(*He indicates the line 'Sunt lacrimae rerum et mentem mortalia tangunt.' Observes that* MAILER *is staring out of the window.*) Perhaps Mailer, who appears to be contemplating his evening's excursion on the boards, will oblige us with a translation.
(*Still looking out of the window* MAILER *obliges. With that slightly Martian precision of his.*)

MAILER: 'Everything is a cause for tears – and the fact that we are mortal cannot be forgotten', sir.

TOMKINSON: (*Dumbstruck*) That's very very good Mailer.
(*Going to him*) May I ask what engaged your attention out there, Mailer?

MAILER: My father, sir. He was outside. Looking up.

TOMKINSON: Oh.
(*Looking down into the street we can see* MR MAILER *looking up.* TOMKINSON *joins* MAILER'S *gaze and the two look down. The master is suddenly embarrassed.*)
Oh. (*A pause.*) Well, carry on.

28. EXT. SCHOOL. DAY
The quadrangle. MAILER *and* JACKSON *are walking out on their way home.* MR POSNER *comes the other way.*
POSNER: Well met by moonlight, Mailer.
MAILER: Yes, sir.
POSNER: Friend Jackson too.
JACKSON: Yes, sir.
POSNER: The costumes are here, Mailer. Is this not exciting?
MAILER: Are they, sir?
POSNER: D.R. tonight.
MAILER: Yes, sir.
POSNER: Mrs Beal will be in charge of them.
MAILER: I know, sir.
POSNER: She asked me to ask you to obtain a brassière.
MAILER: A what, sir?
POSNER: A brassière. I told her that it was extremely unlikely
   that sixteenth-century women wore brassières. I told her
   that brassières were invented in Toledo by a monk in 1629
   but she told me that a brassière was what it required.
MAILER: When I was in the spring play, sir, I just put some
   socks down my front.
POSNER: I remember.
JACKSON: It looked really stupid, sir.
POSNER: Quite. Obtain a brassière from your mum, Mailer,
   and if you like we'll stuff the socks in the brassière. OK?
MAILER: Yes, sir.

29. EXT. SCHOOL. DAY
Outside the school gates. MAILER *and* JACKSON. MAILER *can see his dad on the other side of the road.*
MAILER: Jackson –
JACKSON: Yeah?
MAILER: Keep the other side of me.
JACKSON: Why?
MAILER: It's my dad. I don't want him to see me.

25

JACKSON: Oh. (*His friend's behaviour is puzzling him once again.*)
I thought your dad was OK.
MAILER: None of them are OK. They're all awful.
(*His dad has spotted him and is moving towards him.*)
Run for it.
JACKSON: Mailer –
MAILER: Come on –
(*A chase.* MAILER *and* JACKSON *end up in someone's front garden. His dad runs past. He's missed them. We see him call 'Tony', 'Tony'. Then he gives up and goes back the way he's come.*)
He's no better than she is. I wish they would get divorced. They're both absolutely horrible and I hate them and I wish they were dead.
JACKSON: Come on, Mailer. (*Once again thrown by the violent depths of his friend's character*.) Posner said you were going to be a really good Ophelia.

30. INT. MAILER'S HOUSE. EARLY EVENING
MAILER *has just come home from school. He is loitering on the landing and meets his mother coming from the bedroom.*
MRS MAILER: What are you doing?
MAILER: Nothing. (*Pause.*) I will be a bit late tonight.
MRS MAILER: What's happening then?
MAILER: It's the dress rehearsal. I thought you knew.
(MRS MAILER *looks at him.*)
MRS MAILER: Well, don't be too late, will you.
(MAILER *watches her go downstairs. When he's sure he's safe he goes back into the room and opens the drawer looking for the female garment in question. Finally he gets to the bottom of the drawer. He catches a glimpse of a picture of a little girl. And a whole mass of girl's clothes. Just the brief register of puzzlement and then grabs the bra and stuffs it under his shirt. Goes out. Downstairs his mother is in the hall.*)
Tony. Tony.

26

31. INT. MAILER'S HOUSE. EARLY EVENING

After a while MRS MAILER *gets up as if about to go after the boy but when she gets to the hall can't quite make it. Finally she takes her courage in hand and pulls back the front door calling for the boy but it is not Tony who greets her but her husband. Before she has had time to react he has forced her back into the house.*

MR MAILER: Can I come in?

MRS MAILER: Get out.

MR MAILER: In two minutes.

MRS MAILER: I've told you, I'll call the police.

MR MAILER: Shut it, just shut it. Now, what do you want?

MRS MAILER: What do you think I want?

MR MAILER: You want a divorce? Is that it? We can have a divorce if that's what you want.

MRS MAILER: Thanks . . .

MR MAILER: I'll take Tony off your hands.

(MRS MAILER *laughs.*)

MRS MAILER: Oh, you won't get your hands on Tony. I like little Tony. He's great company is Tony. We talk about Greek and Latin and Shakespeare and we have a great laugh do me and little Tony. Just great.

(*He goes for her.*)

MR MAILER: Listen, you –

MRS MAILER: Ah.

(*And he backs off.*)

Now that's where you make your mistake, isn't it?

(MR MAILER'*s collapsing.*)

You better bloody well sort yourself out, Malcolm, or I will be asking for a divorce. Pretty bloody soon. And you won't come near me or Tony. Ever. You shouldn't be here now.

(MR MAILER'*s taking out an official-looking letter*)

MR MAILER: You talking about this?

MRS MAILER: Yes, I am. And don't try anything because you're not supposed to be within a hundred yards of this place. There's an injunction out on you. (*Taps the letter.*) And if you don't sort yourself out, yes, I am asking for a divorce and pretty bloody soon too. And after that you can kiss goodbye to Tony.

MR MAILER: Please, Mary –

MRS MAILER: How the hell do you think I feel?

MR MAILER: Please. I can't – (*Weak. Then goes cold.*) Jesus.
You're an evil bitch.

MRS MAILER: And what's she then?

MR MAILER: You're just using him. You're just using him to
blackmail me. You don't even like the poor little bastard.
You just –
(*Pause. She is quite immovable.*)

32. INT. SCHOOL. EVENING

In a classroom converted into a dressing room MAILER *is getting into
his Ophelia outfit.* JACKSON *is clad as a soldier and there are
several other boys in costume around. Enter* PATTERSON, *who is
looking highly self-conscious in a black doublet and hose.*

JACKSON: Do you want a hand?

MAILER: No, thanks. Where are they up to?

PATTERSON: First interval. (*Sitting on a desk*) It's no good.

MAILER: What isn't?

PATTERSON: I can't remember the lines.

MAILER: Which lines?

PATTERSON: Any of them. I can't remember any of them.

MAILER: But you've got hundreds of lines. You must be able to
remember some of them.

PATTERSON: Posner'll have to go on. If he can get into this
stupid costume.
(*Enter* SALZBURG, *a fat boy who is playing Gertrude.*)

SALZBURG: I've laddered Mrs Harrison's tights.
(*Enter* MR *and* MRS JACKSON.)

MR JACKSON: Where is the prince of Denmark?

PATTERSON: Here, sir. Patterson – Mod. Six. B.2.

MR JACKSON: 'Now, Hamlet, where's Polonius?'

PATTERSON: Gone to the loo I think, sir.

MR JACKSON: 'At supper? Where?'
(PATTERSON *is completely fazed by this remark.* MR
JACKSON *continues oblivious.*)

28

A few dedicated parents are out there, ravished by the spectacle of Mr Posner's set. It reminds me very forcefully of a Chinese restaurant. Are you all *en chinoiserie*?

PATTERSON: It's actually the same set we used for *The Beggar's Opera*, sir.

JACKSON: I didn't know parents were allowed in for the D.R.

MRS JACKSON: Jimbo.

MR JACKSON: The D.R. The D.R. Exquisite. We who will be unable to watch tomorrow or Saturday, brat, are allowed in to the 'D.R.'.

MRS JACKSON: We're enjoying it very much, Jimbo.
   (MAILER *is now made up.* MR JACKSON *hams in his direction.*)

MR JACKSON: 'Soft you now
   The fair Ophelia! Nymph, in thy orisons
   Be all my sins remember'd.'
   (MAILER, *like the natural actor he is, goes straight into it.*)

MAILER: 'Good my Lord,
   How does your honour for this many a day?'

MR JACKSON: 'I humbly thank you, well.'

MAILER: 'My lord, I have remembrances of yours
   That I have longed long to redeliver.
   I pray you now receive them.'

MR JACKSON: 'No, not I – '

PATTERSON: He's awfully good, isn't he? (*Beaming paternally at* MAILER) If only you could get house colours for acting.

MR JACKSON: Your dad is out there, Mailer.

MAILER: Sorry.

MR JACKSON: Glued to the stage. Fixed.

MRS JACKSON: I think you're a very convincing girl, Tony.
   (*Enter boy in costume plus spear.*)

BOY: My halberd's broken. Has anyone seen Mr Bowles?

JACKSON: He went home.

BOY: You're on, Patterson.

PATTERSON: I'm never off.
   (*Glumly he leaves.*)

29

MR JACKSON: 'The readiness is all', Hamlet. Shall I tell your paterfamilias to come 'out back'?
MAILER: It's all right, Mr Jackson. Thanks.
MR JACKSON: 'Let the doors be shut upon him, that he may play the fool nowhere but in's own house. Farewell.'
   (*And he has gone.* MAILER *turns to* JACKSON.)
JACKSON: Good riddance. Undo me.
MAILER: If he comes up here I won't speak to him. (*Pause.*) I won't. I won't.

33. INT. SCHOOL. EVENING
The stage of Big School. MAILER *comes down into the wings, ready for his entrance. He peers on to the stage where the lead up to the mad scene is being played and then looks down into the auditorium. He sees his father looking up at the stage.*
'QUEEN': 'Let her come in.
   To my sick soul, as sin's true nature is,
   Each toy seems prologue to some great amiss,
   So full of witless jealousy is guilt,
   It spoils itself in fearing to be spoilt.'
'LAERTES': Go on, Mailer. Go on.
   (*We see* MAILER *go on from the wings.*)
MAILER: 'Where is the beauteous Majesty of Denmark?'
'QUEEN': 'How now, Ophelia?'
   (*And* MAILER's *eyes are wandering down to where his father sits.*)
MAILER: (*Sings:*) 'How should I your true love know
      From another one?
   By his cockle hat and staff
      And his sandal shoon.'
'QUEEN': 'Alas, sweet lady, what means this song?'
MAILER: 'Say you? Nay, pray you remember.
   (*Sings:*) He is dead and gone, lady,
      He is dead and gone,
   At his head a grass-grown plot
      At his heels a stone . . .'

(The mishaps in the words are perhaps because MAILER *cannot keep his eyes away from his father.)*

'QUEEN': 'Nay, but Ophelia – '

MAILER: 'Pray you remember.
    (Sings:) White his shroud as was the snow – '
    (Enter the 'KING'.)

'QUEEN': 'Alas, look here, my lord.'

MAILER: *(Sings:)* 'Loaded with sweet flowers
    Which straightway to the grave did go
        With true-love showers.'

'KING': 'How do you, pretty lady?'

MAILER: 'They say the owl was a baker's daughter. Lord, we
    know what we are, but know not what we may be. We – '
    (And he dries. Stares back wildly at the prompt corner.)

PROMPTER: 'God be at your table.'

MAILER: God be what?

PROMPTER: 'God be at your table.'

'KING': 'Conceit upon her father.'
    (And MAILER's *dried again.)*

PROMPTER: 'Pray let's have no words of this.'

MAILER: I can't hear.
    (From the gloom of the auditorium POSNER *rises.)*

POSNER: Are you all right, Mailer?
    *(*MAILER *looks deeply unhappy.)*

MAILER: I can't hear, sir.

POSNER: Go from 'conceit upon her father'.

'KING': 'Conceit upon her father.'
    (But MAILER *stands dumb in the middle of the stage.)*

PROMPTER: 'Pray let's have no words of this.'

MAILER: I can't, sir. *(Near to tears)* I'm sorry, sir. I can't, sir.
    I'm sorry.

POSNER: Mailer –

MAILER: I'm sorry, sir –
    (He's backing off the stage. His father rises.)

MR MAILER: Tony –
    (But he's gone.)

PATTERSON: Is he all right, sir, do you think?

POSNER: Go on, boy, after him.
MR MAILER: Tony –

34. INT. SCHOOL. NIGHT

MAILER *has run back into the school, sobbing. The cast,* POSNER *and his father chase him, across the balcony behind Big School and along the grim-looking corridor. We see him run into an empty classroom and shut the door as* MR MAILER, *followed by the cast and* POSNER, *stops.* PATTERSON *is in fact the only one up with him. Other boys are at the back, hesitant and suddenly scared in their costumes.* MR MAILER *speaks gently to* PATTERSON.

MR MAILER: You go back, son.
PATTERSON: Is he all right, sir?
MR MAILER: I don't know.
PATTERSON: He takes acting awfully seriously.
POSNER: Patterson –
PATTERSON: Yes, sir.
  (*As he goes back* MR MAILER *goes on towards the classroom where his son is hiding.*)
POSNER: Do you want me to –
MR MAILER: No, I'll be fine. Honest.
POSNER: Are you sure?
MR MAILER: Yeah.
  (*And Dad is tapping at the heavy door of the classroom. And after a while the door opens, and, watched by the company,* MR MAILER *goes in to his younger son.*)

35. INT. SCHOOL. NIGHT
In the classroom.
MR MAILER: It's freezing in here.
MAILER: Yes.
MR MAILER: Did you open that window?
MAILER: Yes.
MR MAILER: Now, what would you want to go and do a thing like that for?
MAILER: There was a boy who threw himself out of a window.
MR MAILER: Yeah? Where was this then?

MAILER: At a school. I read about it in the paper.

MR MAILER: Yeah? Well. Now you wouldn't want to do anything like that, would you?

MAILER: (*Takes wig off*) Why didn't you come?

MR MAILER: . . . Well . . . I . . .

MAILER: You said you'd come and get me.

MR MAILER: Well, it was stupid of me to say that. Tony, if I'd taken you away I'd never get to keep you. D'you see? They'd find me and I'd never get you.

MAILER: I don't understand.

MR MAILER: Well . . . it's the law . . . this injunction business, it . . . Listen, I don't understand it myself really but . . . Well, I tell you this.

MAILER: What?

MR MAILER: That if you want to live with me you shall.

MAILER: Oh.

MR MAILER: We just have to be careful about it, that's all. You know . . . your mother.

MAILER: I hate her.

MR MAILER: You mustn't say that.

MAILER: But I do. She hits me. She says I'm a baby. She says I'm a snob. She's going to take me away from the school . . . Why is she so horrid to me?

MR MAILER: Well, she . . . if I could just explain to you why she's the way she is . . . I'd . . . but I dunno.

MAILER: Well, it's all right if I can live with you, I suppose.

MR MAILER: Hey . . . Y'know you're very good at this stuff . . . I mean, really good.

MAILER: I shouldn't have run out like that, I feel awfully ashamed.

MR MAILER: Aaah, come on. You don't worry about that. You'll be fine . . . fine. Er, listen . . . I think they're waiting.

MAILER: I better go back.

MR MAILER: That's the stuff. I'll see you later and we'll talk, eh?

MAILER: Yes . . . all right.

33

MR MAILER: Good . . . Come on.
(*They move to the door.*)

36. INT. SCHOOL. NIGHT
MAILER *walks towards the others. And* POSNER *steps out.*
MAILER: I'm sorry, Mr Posner.
POSNER: I – (*Suddenly sees the only way to get him out of this is by acting through it. Bows low.*) 'I hope all will be well. We must be patient.'
MAILER: 'We must be patient.'
POSNER: 'But – '
(*And the boy's confidence is returning. This is one thing he can do with his whole soul.*)
MAILER: 'But I cannot choose but weep to think they would lay him i'th' cold ground.'
(*And now he is Ophelia. No problem. The court parts to let him through.*)
'My brother shall know of it. And so I thank you for your good counsel. Come, my coach! Good night, ladies, good night. Sweet ladies, good night, good night . . .'
(*And his dad calls to him.*)
MR MAILER: Give 'em hell, Tony . . .
(MAILER *turns. Distracted. Not yet down from being a princess. Then suddenly he is a small, unhappy boy again.*)
MAILER: Yes. Dad. Yes.
(*His father watches, tears at the back of his eyes as the boy goes off with* POSNER'*s arm round him and the hubbub of the play starts again.*)
POSNER: Right, we were going to go from Ophelia's entry – 'So full of artless jealousy'.

34

EPISODE TWO
Day 17. Wednesday, 23 October 1985

1. INT. SCHOOL. NIGHT
The school theatre. The curtain call after Hamlet. MR MAILER
clapping in the audience.

2. EXT. STREET. NIGHT
Mr Mailer's car draws up outside Mailer's house. And MAILER *is
getting out of the car.*
MR MAILER: Look. Don't wind her up, that's all.
MAILER: She picks on me. She always picks on me.
MR MAILER: I'll get it sorted.
MAILER: It's worse if you're not there.
MR MAILER: I'll think of something. Honest.
MAILER: All right.
MR MAILER: Go on now. You run along. It will be all right.

3. INT./EXT. MAILER'S HOUSE. NIGHT
MRS MAILER *opens the door to* MAILER. *She looks out at the street
beyond him but sees no sign of Mr Mailer's car.*
MRS MAILER: Finished then?
MAILER: You didn't come.
> (*They go inside the hall. A car comes back down the street. Mr
> Mailer's.* MAILER *half turns. She notices the reaction but does
> not follow it up.*)

Day 22. Monday, 28 October

4. EXT. SCHOOL. DAY
JACKSON *and* MAILER *in the goal mouth. The rest of the players
are at the other end of the pitch. It is not a particularly distinguished
collection of players.*
MAILER: I was reading a book on it.
JACKSON: Yes.
MAILER: It's rather complicated.
> (*A small Jewish boy called* SAMUELSON *approaches them.
> Wise and cynical for his years. They look back up the pitch and*

35

*it is indeed awful. A desultory scramble for this is the weeds
and wets game. He goes morosely back up the pitch.*)
Apparently this book said one of them gets custody
apparently.

JACKSON: I know.

MAILER: If they're a fit parent.

JACKSON: No such thing as a fit parent.

MAILER: Well, she isn't a fit parent, is she? She's a loony. She
should be in a bin. (*Pause.*) I'm going to expose her.

JACKSON: Well, the thing about my parents –
(*He is not particularly interested in* MAILER'*s problems. Their
discussion is interrupted by* PATTERSON, *who arrives complete
with whistle and flash running shorts.*)

PATTERSON: Mailer, what are you doing at this end of the
pitch?

MAILER: I'm defending Jackson.

PATTERSON: Against what?

MAILER: Against attack, Patterson.

PATTERSON: Mailer, there is no attack. All your team are at the
other end. They are all at the other end of the pitch. And
the opposing team are there too. You are not defending
Jackson. You are talking to him.

MAILER: I'm talking to him and defending him . . .
(*They look up and a shambolic line of players is running up the
pitch towards them. The ball rolling listlessly ahead of them.*)
Look. Here comes an attack.

PATTERSON: Game Eight is ludicrous actually. Ludicrous. You
shouldn't be allowed to play football.

JACKSON: Rothermere let us all go to the cinema once.

PATTERSON: Oh my *God* –
(PATTERSON *has realized that almost the entire red team is
offside. He runs towards them blowing his whistle and yelling.*)

5. INT. SCHOOL. DAY
When he gets to the desk, POSNER, *who, by the way, like all the
masters in this school, is in academic gown, nods to* MAILER *and
they go out into the corridor. The door of the classroom is still open*

36

and we can see the business of the house being still transacted.

POSNER: Mailer, could I see you a moment? How are things at
home, boy?

MAILER: All right, sir.

POSNER: Good. Good. (*Awkward*) How's your dad?

MAILER: Fine, sir.

POSNER: Good. Good. (*Putting his arm round* MAILER *and
taking him away down the corridor*) I wanted to ask you
something, boy. Man to man.

MAILER: Yes, sir.

(MAILER *is excruciatingly embarrassed. Under the illusion this
is to be something about his father and mother.*)

POSNER: You see . . . Bejam's voice is breaking.

MAILER: Yes, sir.

POSNER: And he is the Virgin Mary.

MAILER: Yes, sir.

POSNER: It would be quite a lot of work.

MAILER: What would, sir?

POSNER: You being it.

MAILER: Being what, sir?

POSNER: The . . . er . . . Virgin Mary.

MAILER: Oh.

(*They have arrived at the end of the corridor. Looking down at
the main hall. Boys chasing each other, shouting.*)

I don't think I want to play any more girls, sir.

POSNER: Mailer, this isn't any old rubbish. This isn't any old
Virgin. This is the Virgin. The *echt* and original Virgin. It's
an awfully good part. Jesus's Mum.

MAILER: Couldn't Samuelson or Zwemmer do it, sir?

POSNER: Mailer, both the boys you mention are of the Jewish
faith. I don't think it would be quite proper for either of
them to play the Virgin Mary. I think it would be excellent
if they were involved in some capacity. Possibly being the
lighting or –

MAILER: But she was Jewish, wasn't she, sir?

(POSNER *looks down at him sharply. Is* MAILER *being
insolent? No. Merely extremely intelligent. He puts his arm*

37

round the boy and they walk back towards the classroom.)

POSNER: Mailer, I obviously can't force you to play the part. Mailer – but I am a bit pushed. The only other candidate is Gellhorn Minor.

MAILER: Yes, sir.

POSNER: You see the dimensions of the problem.

MAILER: Yes, sir.

POSNER: I've given her some awfully good lines. She has an extra speech foretelling the fall of the Roman Empire.

MAILER: Really, sir?

POSNER: Hooked already.

MAILER: Yes, sir.

(PATTERSON *emerges from the meeting.*)

POSNER: Patterson's signed up, aren't you, Patterson?

PATTERSON: For what, sir?

POSNER: He plays a tax collector. Don't you, Patterson?

PATTERSON: Sorry, sir?

(POSNER *winks at* MAILER *as he moves away.*)

POSNER: Give my best to your father, Mailer. All my best.

6. INT. MAILER'S HOUSE. NIGHT

MAILER *coming into his house. He lets himself in. Stops in the hall and calls out 'Hullo.' No answer. Goes on upstairs. No one around. Finally he goes into his mother's room. He opens the top drawer of her cupboard. Going through her clothes he takes from under his shirt the bra and carefully replaces it at the bottom of the drawer. As in Episode One he sees again the photograph of a little girl but on the back it says 'Alison' and* MAILER *does turn over the picture wonderingly. Then* MAILER *freezes. He has heard something. Puts it back exactly as he found it. Goes to the top of the stairs. There below him is his mother, laden with shopping. She stops.*

MRS MAILER: Oh. (*Pause.*) You're back. Are you coming down – I need to talk to you.

7. INT. MAILER'S HOUSE. NIGHT

MAILER *and his mum in the kitchen.*

MRS MAILER: I don't think I've been very well, Tony. I should

38

have talked to you. It's just that it's much easier since he left.

MAILER: Why?

MRS MAILER: I can't explain it, Tony. I can't explain it to you.

MAILER: Why don't you like him, Mum?

MRS MAILER: It's him, lovey. He doesn't like me.

MAILER: Oh.

MRS MAILER: Look. You and that school.

MAILER: Can I stay there?

MRS MAILER: For God's sake – (*But she controls herself.*) Yes. Yes, you can. (*Pause.*) He'll just have to pay, that's all.

MAILER: Thanks . . .

MRS MAILER: It was the money. We argued about it. All the time. (*Pause.*) I'm going to get a divorce, I've decided. It's the only way.

MAILER: Yes, he –

(*He stops himself just in time. He has had to learn to control what he says. She looks up.*)

MRS MAILER: He what?

MAILER: He has a . . . girlfriend. John told me.

MRS MAILER: Oh.

MAILER: Does he spend it on her?

MRS MAILER: Oh, Tony. This is all wrong. All wrong.

MAILER: Is she young?

MRS MAILER: She's as old as me.

(MRS MAILER *is in tears.* MAILER *doesn't know what to do.*) I'm sorry, Tony. I've not been well.

MAILER: Thank you for letting me stay at the school.

MRS MAILER: Tell me what you did today.

MAILER: Football in the afternoon. I'm awful.

MRS MAILER: Yes?

MAILER: And . . .

(*She's holding his hand. He is understandably confused.*) Is that why you were so cross all the time?

MRS MAILER: Yes. Yes, I was a bit . . .

(*She taps the side of her head.*)

MAILER: Bonkers.

39

MRS MAILER: Yeah.
(MAILER *and* MRS MAILER *are both laughing.*)
It's better now he's . . . now he's . . . (*Holds on to herself, not to get hysterical.*) Anyway I got some happy pills.
MAILER: Tranquillizers.
MRS MAILER: That's it. Happy pills for when you're sad.
MAILER: Dad said the other day I –
MRS MAILER: Has he been to see you?
MAILER: I –
MRS MAILER: Has he?
MAILER: No. (*Pause.*) No.
MRS MAILER: Tell me if he does, lovey, won't you?
MAILER: Why?
MRS MAILER: I have to know, you see.
(MRS MAILER *goes through into the kitchen. She comes to the door, watching him shrewdly.*)
Has he been telling you something? You can tell me. I won't mind.
MAILER: He said not to tell you.
MRS MAILER: Did he say I'd be angry? I bet he did.
MAILER: He –
MRS MAILER: He came to see you, didn't he?
MAILER: He came to see the play.
MRS MAILER: Yes.
(*Pause.* MAILER *is miserable at all this.*)
MAILER: Why didn't you come and see the play?
MRS MAILER: I told you, lovey. That school. It scares me stiff. It looks like a bloody cathedral. It – I'm not angry.
(*Coming into the room and going to her son*) What did he say to you? Did he say bad things about me?
MAILER: No.
MRS MAILER: Are you sure now?
MAILER: He didn't.
MRS MAILER: I won't mind.
MAILER: He said it might have to be a divorce.
MRS MAILER: It's not me. It's him.
MAILER: Oh.

(*She's watching him. He's still not entirely sure of her.*)

MRS MAILER: He's not supposed to see you, you see. (*Goes back into the kitchen.*) I was thinking the other day about how it was before all this started. When we went to Broadstairs. Do you remember? And you played with Mrs Stimpson's chair? Do you remember? The nice times. Do you remember the nice times?

MAILER: Yes, I do.

MRS MAILER: Look.

(*When she's checked the tea she comes back in to him over the next dialogue.*)

There's someone coming to see you. To ask all sorts of questions. Because of something your father's done.

MAILER: What questions?

MRS MAILER: Your father's done something very wicked and stupid.

MAILER: What's he done?

MRS MAILER: He wants to take you away from me.

MAILER: Is this custody?

MRS MAILER: Oh God, what do they teach you at that school?

MAILER: Do you want custody? Is that what it's all about? Is that what you're arguing about?

(*His mother is near to tears.*)

MRS MAILER: It means he'd have you all the time. Do you see? I wouldn't get a look in.

(*The significance of this is lost on* MAILER.)

I'm sorry. I don't deserve you. I don't have any rights over you. I'm sorry. I'm so sorry. I love you so much. I'm sorry.

(*He doesn't move.*)

Please just come and hold my hand.

(*He still doesn't move.*)

Please.

(*And finally he goes to her.*)

Oh darling.

(*She kisses him.*)

Oh love.

Day 27. Saturday, 2 November

8. INT. JACKSON'S HOUSE. EVENING
Jackson's bedroom, a room much decorated with R. & B. posters.
JACKSON *is at the mirror.* JACKSON *and* MAILER *are in 'going out'*
gear. JACKSON's *very Carnaby Street and* MAILER *is a little bit*
inclined to the sports jacket approach.
MAILER: Actually –
JACKSON: Yes.
MAILER: I think they're both loony. You can't believe a word
  either of them say.
JACKSON: What do you think of the jacket?
MAILER: It's amazingly good.
  (*Enter* MR JACKSON, *dramatically.*)
MR JACKSON: Heaven and all the angels, Jimbo. I find Mailer's
  tweeds more appropriate. Mailer looks quite Edwardian.
MAILER: I don't go to these parties. This is my first one in fact.
MR JACKSON: Back by eleven, Jimbo.
  (*He goes.*)
JACKSON: God, I hate him. God. (*Pause.*) Jimbo. Fancy calling
  me Jimbo.
MAILER: If you could choose which one you'd live with – who
  would you choose?
JACKSON: Her, I suppose. (*Throws himself on to the bed.*) I am
  sure all the criminals he defends go to prison for hundreds
  and hundreds of years. He's completely useless at
  everything is my Dad. (*Watching* MAILER) Which one are
  you going with?
MAILER: She's trying to get round me. But I know what she's
  doing. I'm going to tell someone about her.
JACKSON: What are you going to tell them about her?
MAILER: I think she's got another kid somewhere. A girl. I
  found a picture in her drawer, of a girl called Alison. It was
  really strange.
JACKSON: Really. What –

(*The door opens dramatically and* MR JACKSON *shows in* HUGHES.)

MR JACKSON: Hughes arrives.

(HUGHES *carries two bottles of cider and wears a trilby. He seems more than usually eager and hairy.*)

HUGHES: I've got the address. Six Hadstock Lane. Say you're friends of Jackie's. Do you like the hat?

9. EXT. JACKSON'S HOUSE. EVENING

HUGHES, JACKSON *and* MAILER *coming out into the road under the watchful eye of* MR JACKSON.

MR JACKSON: May we know who is going to this party?

HUGHES: We've just got an address, Mr Jackson. *In* fact we've got three addresses.

MR JACKSON: And what do you propose to *do* at this party?

HUGHES: Dance. (*Pause.*) If we get in.

MR JACKSON: You may not get in?

HUGHES: Sometimes we don't get in.

MR JACKSON: I'm sure they'll let Mailer in. Mailer looks a real toff.

MAILER: Thanks, Mr Jackson.

MR JACKSON: Off you go then. Eleven, Jimbo.

(*They go down the path. At the bottom of the path* MAILER *stops.*)

MAILER: I think I should have worn my polo neck.

JACKSON: You what?

MAILER: My polo neck. This jacket's awful.

HUGHES: It's a great jacket.

MAILER: I think I'll change.

JACKSON: If he likes it there must be something wrong with it.

MAILER: I'll catch you up.

HUGHES: Tell you what . . . (*Sensing that* MAILER *is not as confident as they are*) I'll lend you my hat. It'll go with a polo neck.

MAILER: Thanks, Hughes. Wait for me at the bus stop.

JACKSON: See you.

(*And they go off down the street.*)

43

10. EXT./INT. MAILER'S HOUSE. EVENING

MAILER *runs back to his house and we see him duck through the side entrance. As he passes through he hears voices. Stops. It is his mother and father.*

MR MAILER: (*Out of shot*) Then why did you let me in?

MRS MAILER: (*Out of shot*) Because –

(*He goes to the window and the scene is played with* MAILER *watching from the darkness. A painful scene of adult confrontation.*)

MR MAILER: It's happening, Mary, the lawyers are going ahead with it, it is happening, you can't actually stop it.

MRS MAILER: All I meant was that –

MR MAILER: Well, why did your lawyers write me that letter, eh? Why? I presume they meant what they said.

MRS MAILER: You shouldn't have made the boy the issue.

MR MAILER: What else could I do? I'm not supposed to go near him. I'm not supposed to be here now. The boy is the issue as far as I'm concerned.

MRS MAILER: It's funny, since you've left I've been able to talk to him.

(MAILER *runs off down the street.*)

MR MAILER: Can I get my things? Please.

MRS MAILER: I don't want this, Malcolm.

MR MAILER: Then why did you write the letter?

MRS MAILER: Because you hurt me. You hurt me so much. And I want to hurt you. It's not fair I should be the one that's hurt. It's not fair.

(*He walks past her.*)

11. EXT. STREET. EVENING

By now MAILER *has turned and run out into the street and not stopped till he reaches his friends at the bus stop.*

12. EXT. STREET. EVENING

MAILER *panting up to the bus stop.*

JACKSON: You didn't change?

MAILER: No. (*Self-conscious*) I think the jacket's OK. It really makes me look older I think.

HUGHES: Actually –

MAILER: What?

HUGHES: Could I have my hat back?

MAILER: Of course.

(*Under the watchful eye of an adult they wait like good public schoolboys for their bus.*)

Will there be lots of girls there?

HUGHES: Loads. (*Jigging around self-consciously body-popping*) And they all . . . you know . . .

MAILER: Yeah?

HUGHES: Yeah. Oh yeah.

13. INT. MAILER'S HOUSE. EVENING

MR MAILER is in the bedroom, gathering his things from the drawers and slamming them into a suitcase.

MR MAILER: Oh Jesus.

MRS MAILER: What's the matter?

MR MAILER: Do you have to?

MRS MAILER: It's nothing to do with you.

MR MAILER: Alison isn't anything to do with me?

MRS MAILER: She –

(*He rounds on her.*)

MR MAILER: You're bloody sick, Mary, and until you get that into your head we'll never get together. Ever!

MRS MAILER: (*As he goes*) Don't go! Please! Please!

14. EXT. SUBURBAN HOUSE. NIGHT

Outside the party. A respectable suburban house full to bursting. A BOY *is holding open the door while behind him we perceive signs of revelry.* HUGHES *is batting for the lads.*

HUGHES: I'm a friend of Jackie's.

BOY: Jackie who?

HUGHES: Jackie Bergman. It's her party, isn't it?

BOY: And Julie Welch Carpenter's. And Kate Minchin Smith, in fact. (*Suspicious*) What colour hair has she got?

HUGHES: Black.

BOY: All right. But you've got to have some girls before you come in.

HUGHES: Aren't there any girls in there?

BOY: Hundreds. But we want more.

(*He slams the door.*)

HUGHES: Bastards – let's go round the back.

(*They go off carrying the bottles of cider round the side of the house and into the back garden. They knock on the back door. This door is slammed.*)

JACKSON: Where's the other address?

HUGHES: Swiss Cottage. Say you're friends of Kevin Taylor Walker's. It doesn't sound very good. We're friends of Jackie's.

SECOND BOY: Jackie who?

HUGHES: Jackie Bergman.

SECOND BOY: Never heard of her.

(*They look in the back window. Here they are looking into the kitchen. Crowded with rather glum-looking boys.*)

JACKSON: Doesn't look much of a party.

MAILER: I'll tell you what. Let's drink the cider. Here.

JACKSON: What a brilliant idea.

MAILER: Sort of in someone else's back garden.

15. INT. BUS. NIGHT

The bus going home. MAILER *is sitting with his head in his hands.*

JACKSON: Do you want to be sick again?

MAILER: Not yet.

JACKSON: Look, stick your fingers down your throat.

CONDUCTOR: If he's going to do it he can get off this bus.

JACKSON: All right.

MAILER: She'll kill me when I get home. (*In utter misery*) I've never been drunk before.

JACKSON: Are you still drunk?

MAILER: I don't know if I was ever actually drunk. I just felt peculiar.

HUGHES: I've got a great address next week. In Barnet.

16. EXT./INT. MAILER'S HOUSE. NIGHT

MAILER *coming up to his front door, trying to compose himself desperately. He rings the bell. His mum answers.*

MRS MAILER: What's up with you?

MAILER: Nothing.

MRS MAILER: What are you looking like that for?

MAILER: I feel a bit funny.

MRS MAILER: Have you been drinking?

MAILER: I had some cider.

MRS MAILER: How much?

MAILER: Some bottles. (*Pause.*) I think I'm going to be sick.

MRS MAILER: Oh God help us all.

17. INT. MAILER'S HOUSE. NIGHT

MAILER *in his mum's bedroom.* MRS MAILER *is undressing him.* MAILER *is quite gone.*

MRS MAILER: When I was your age I had loads of boyfriends.

MAILER: Did you?

MRS MAILER: Loads.

MAILER: Is that when you met Dad?

MRS MAILER: No. (*Pause.*) Lift your feet up.

MAILER: What's she like, this girl he's got?

MRS MAILER: She's not a very nice person.

MAILER: If I lived with him, would she be there all the time?

MRS MAILER: Oh yes.

MAILER: I've never seen her.

MRS MAILER: No. (*Pause.*) Well, I've never seen her either. She was kept a secret, you see. Until quite recently. (*She is slightly unnerved by his shrewdness.*)

MAILER: When people get divorced do they ever get married again?

MRS MAILER: Not very often.

MAILER: There wouldn't be much point, would there? (*Pause.*) Mrs Jackson's very nice.

MRS MAILER: Is she?

MAILER: Very nice. She makes these sort of flapjacks.

MRS MAILER: Are they better than mine then?

47

MAILER: Er . . . (*Pause.*) I'm sorry, Mum.

MRS MAILER: That's all right, lovey.

MAILER: Mum –

MRS MAILER: Yeah?

MAILER: Who's Alison?

MRS MAILER: Sorry?

MAILER: Who's Alison?

(MRS MAILER *doesn't answer this one. He falls asleep. When he is asleep his mother goes to the cupboard and gets out the clothes. Lowers them on to the bed next to him. They are the girl's clothes we saw in the drawer earlier. She goes back to the cupboard and takes out more girl's clothes.* MRS MAILER *spreads the clothes across the bed and the little boy turns over into them in his sleep. She bends over him and kisses him passionately. She goes out.*)

18. INT./EXT. MAILER'S HOUSE. NIGHT

MRS MAILER *sitting alone in the kitchen. From the road the lights of a car approaching. She goes to the curtains and peers out. The car stops and out comes* JOHN. MRS MAILER, *very excited, runs to the door.* JOHN *sees her as she is coming down the path.*

JOHN: Hello, Mum.

MRS MAILER: What happened?

JOHN: I came home.

MRS MAILER: I can see.

JOHN: I'm getting married, Mum.

MRS MAILER: Oh . . . (*Pause.*) Oh . . . (*Pause.*) That's wonderful.

Day 28. Sunday, 3 November

19. INT. MAILER'S HOUSE. DAY

Breakfast in the dining room. MAILER *and* JOHN *are at a table.*

MAILER: They both want custody apparently.

JOHN: Stone me.

(*Enter* MRS MAILER.)

MRS MAILER: Have you told him yet?

48

JOHN: What? Oh, that.
MRS MAILER: He's getting married.
MAILER: Who to?
MRS MAILER: Her name's Terry apparently.
MAILER: Is she nice?
JOHN: You'll love her.
MRS MAILER: Her picture looked nice. I think it's exciting.
Don't you, Tony?
(MRS MAILER *goes out to the kitchen.*)
MAILER: (*To* JOHN) How long have you known her?
JOHN: Three weeks.
MAILER: Isn't that rather quick?
JOHN: I don't know.
MAILER: Is she pregnant?
JOHN: Give me a chance, genius.
MAILER: I'm not a genius. Was there a lot of slippery in
France?
(JOHN *cuffs him.* JOHN *gestures towards the kitchen.*)

Day 31. Wednesday, 6 November

20. EXT./INT. COACH. DAY
A coach which carries members of the school Cadet Force. MAILER
and JACKSON *are climbing aboard, closely pursued by* KITCHEN,
their Platoon Sergeant.
MAILER: Some of them are getting married and the rest are
getting divorced. It's ridiculous really.
JACKSON: I'd quite like a brother.
MAILER: Brothers aren't bad in a way.
JACKSON: I think they'd leave me alone if I had a brother.
MAILER: Mailer.
JACKSON: Jackson.
(*They get to their seats in the coach and* KITCHEN *marches in
behind. The coach moves off.*)

21. INT. COACH. DAY

KITCHEN: Here is a typical rifle. I'm going to give you again a simple mnemonic to help you remember what not to do with the rifle.

JACKSON: Kitchen.

KITCHEN: But before I do give you the mnemonic – does anyone remember it?

(*Silence*.)

MAILER: Is this the mnemonic to help you remember not to point the gun at people, sir?

KITCHEN: On the right line – now does anyone remember what that mnemonic is?

SAMUELSON: Is it –

KITCHEN: Yes, Private Samuelson –

SAMUELSON: Is it EGOLAPSCW, Kitchen?

KITCHEN: EGOLAPSCW refers to Enemy Ground Own Troops, etc., doesn't it? We're looking for BRCKKS – like in Aristophanes' *The Frogs* – Breech Rifles Can Kill For Sure For Sure. Mnemonics are there to help you. OK?

PLATOON: Aye aye, Serg.

22. EXT. PIRBRIGHT. DAY

JACKSON *and* MAILER *are crawling through the undergrowth.*

MAILER: What I'd really like to do is to come and live at your house until they sort it all out.

JACKSON: So when do you think she had this illegitimate baby then?

MAILER: Oh years ago. (*Pause*.) And I think he made her give it away.

JACKSON: It sounds amazing.

MAILER: Don't you believe me?

JACKSON: Oh of course I believe you . . .

(*Once again that suggestion that he is unable to deal with his friend's problems.* KITCHEN *crawls up to them with elaborate circumspection.*)

KITCHEN: Now, Mailer – we're doing the leopard crawl now, but we're coming up to a bare ridge. What will we do then,

50

do you think?

MAILER: Er – (*Pause.*) The monkey run, Kitchen.

KITCHEN: Correct, Mailer. We will be going WSW along the perimeter of Red territory and we will be using the monkey run, which is what, Jackson?

JACKSON: Knees and knuckles, Kitchen.

KITCHEN: Excellent. I'll just take a look-see.
(*He lifts up his head and there is a fusillade of rifle fire.*)
Oh, my God.
(*The firing continues.*)
Stop firing there. You're against the skyline.
(*He gets up. Firing continues.* KITCHEN *waves his hands.*)
Stop firing, Reds!

JACKSON: If this was a real war we'd all be dead.

MAILER: Kitchen'd be court-martialled.
(*And, as the firing continues from Red territory, another group of keen young amateur soldiers descends upon them, howling and blasting.* MAILER *and* JACKSON *and* KITCHEN *well and truly blasted.*)

KITCHEN: *No no no no no! Who said you could attack? Who said, eh? You're not supposed to!*

23. EXT. STREET. EVENING
MAILER *and* JACKSON *coming up towards their respective houses.* MAILER *looks as if he has just come out of the Okinawa landings.*

JACKSON: See you tomorrow.

MAILER: See you.
(*But he loiters by Jackson's house. He doesn't really want to go home.*)

JACKSON: Come in if you like.

MAILER: I ought to get back.

JACKSON: I don't think they'd mind.

MAILER: No. I'm always coming round to your house, aren't I?

JACKSON: Well . . . (*Awkward pause.*) Sometimes you're a bit . . .

MAILER: A bit what?

JACKSON: You know.
MAILER: Sorry.
  (*He continues up the street.*)
  See you.
  (*And he continues up the street to his house.*)

24. INT. MAILER'S HOUSE. EVENING
The kitchen.
MRS MAILER: What happened to you?
MAILER: I got ambushed.
MRS MAILER: There's a lady here to see you. From the Social
  Services.
MAILER: Oh.
MRS MAILER: You were late.
MAILER: I was ambushed. I told you.
MRS MAILER: Oh God. You do look a mess.
  (*They go into the hall.*)
MAILER: Shall I change?
MRS MAILER: She's been here ages.
MAILER: Oh. (*Pause.*) Shall I go and see her then?
MRS MAILER: Would you mind?
MAILER: No. I don't mind.
MRS MAILER: She'll ask you questions about me.
MAILER: Oh.
  (*Pause.*)
MRS MAILER: It's been nice, hasn't it?
MAILER: What has?
MRS MAILER: Since he went. Hasn't it been nice?
MAILER: Yes. (*Pause.*) Why doesn't he ever come back?
MRS MAILER: Lovey, she'll ask you all about me.
MAILER: I won't say you're horrible.
MRS MAILER: That's my love.
MAILER: You're not horrible.
MRS MAILER: No. (*Hugs him.*) Just a few questions, that's all.
  (*Round the corner from the front room comes the social worker,*
  CLARE, *a dumpy sensible girl in her mid-thirties.*)

25. INT. MAILER'S HOUSE. EVENING

MAILER *and* MRS MAILER *and* CLARE *in the front room.*

CLARE: And which team are you in?

MAILER: We don't have teams.

CLARE: Oh.

MAILER: We have armies. A Red army and a Blue army.

CLARE: And are you Red or Blue?

MAILER: I was Blue. Today.
    (*Pause.*)

CLARE: Mrs Mailer, I wonder if you'd mind if I –

MRS MAILER: If you what?

CLARE: If I talked to Tony . . .

MAILER: Where?

CLARE: On his own.

MRS MAILER: Oh. (*Pause.*) Oh. (*Pause.*)

MAILER: What about?

MRS MAILER: Oh, of course that's fine. Fine. (*Nervous grin.*)
    Won't be a moment.

CLARE: No.

MRS MAILER: OK, Tony?

CLARE: It'll just be easier to . . . you know . . . talk . . .

MRS MAILER: Yes. (*As she's backing out*) Yes.
    (*After she's gone there is an immensely long pause.*)

CLARE: Well. (*Pause.*) And who won – the Red army or the
    Blue army?
    (TONY *looks at her. There is no answer. Only a pause that no
    one seems able to fill. The two stare at each other in silence.*)

26. INT. MAILER'S HOUSE. EVENING

MRS MAILER *pacing in the kitchen.* CLARE *comes out eventually.*

CLARE: Mrs Mailer?

MRS MAILER: Well, did he say anything?

CLARE: Not much.

MRS MAILER: No. (*Pause.*) Well, he's not a talkative boy.
    (*Pause.*)

CLARE: Well, he didn't say much to me.

MRS MAILER: Oh.

CLARE: I think he's very confused.

MRS MAILER: Well, you would be, wouldn't you?

CLARE: Mrs Mailer, I know this may seem to be an impertinent question, but is everything between you and your husband irreparable?

MRS MAILER: Well, you've seen him.

CLARE: Yes.

MRS MAILER: I don't know. (*Pause.*) Sometimes it feels as if it is. And sometimes it doesn't. Each day is different. (*Pause.*) But most days it feels . . . dead. You know? (*Crying*) It's awful.

CLARE: Please . . .

MRS MAILER: I'm sorry.

CLARE: It's all right.

MRS MAILER: It's like someone's died.

CLARE: I'm sorry . . .

MRS MAILER: I go over it and over it and –

CLARE: What?

MRS MAILER: I suppose I hoped . . .

CLARE: That what?

MRS MAILER: That he'd come to his senses. But it just got . . . That woman . . . While he's with that woman I can't . . . (MAILER *comes into the kitchen.*)

MAILER: Can I have my tea now? *I'm* starving.

Day 39. Thursday, 14 November

27. INT. SWIMMING POOL. DAY

MAILER *and* JACKSON *are poised by the side of the pool waiting for instructions.*

JACKSON: Can you come to tea on Saturday?

MAILER: That would have been great. But I've got to see my probation officer.

JACKSON: Have you got a probation officer?

MAILER: Yeah.

JACKSON: How amazing. (*Pause.*) Why?

MAILER: She decides which one I live with, I think. Actually,

54

it's really awful. The two of them never stop going on and I
don't know –
(*He realizes* JACKSON *is not listening.* JACKSON *joins*
HUGHES *who is standing some distance from them.* MAILER
comes up to them. Silence. Then:)
HUGHES: I've got a great address for Saturday.
JACKSON: Where?
HUGHES: It's in Devon.

Day 41. Saturday, 16 November

28. INT. STAIRS. DAY
MAILER *and* CLARE *going up the stairs to the flat where his father
is living.*
CLARE: Have you ever been here before?
MAILER: No.
CLARE: And how long has Daddy been away now?
MAILER: A week or so. I don't know really. A month, is it? I
    don't know.
CLARE: It's almost nearer two months, I think.
    (*She is trying, in a reasonably subtle way, to assess the damage.
    But* MAILER *is a hard boy to get through to.* CLARE *reverts to
    a bright, professional manner.*)
MAILER: Will Marcia be here?
    (MAILER *and* CLARE *have reached the door of the flat, on a
    dingy-looking landing*)
CLARE: Who's Marcia?
MAILER: His girlfriend.
CLARE: Ah.
MAILER: My brother John said she was a right tart and he
    wasn't having her come to the wedding.
CLARE: Which wedding was that?
MAILER: His wedding.
CLARE: Oh.
    (*She has pressed the bell. The door opens. It is Mailer's Dad.*)
MR MAILER: Hullo, son.
MAILER: Hullo.

(*They kiss.*)

CLARE: Hello again, Mr Mailer. (*Pause.*) Is it nice to see your
  dad again?

MAILER: Yes. It is.

MR MAILER: You'd better come in.

CLARE: Thanks.

29. INT. FLAT. DAY

The flat is surprisingly cosy and looked after.

CLARE: Is this your flat, Mr Mailer?

MR MAILER: No. It's a friend's.

CLARE: Ah. (*Pause.*) A friend from work, is that right?

MR MAILER: That's right.

CLARE: And you live here alone?

MR MAILER: That's it.

CLARE: You sure?

MR MAILER: Look under the bed. (*Pause.*) Can I talk to the
  boy? I got him a present.

MAILER: What was it?

CLARE: It's just that we have been given the impression that
  you live here with someone.

MR MAILER: I wonder who's given you that impression.
  (MAILER *goes.*)

CLARE: I'm simply having to ask some factual questions.

MR MAILER: There's just me lives here. If you go in there, boy,
  you'll find something on the bed.

MAILER: OK.

CLARE: Mr Mailer, you do understand my position?

MR MAILER: I don't want the boy upset. I don't want that. But
  . . . (*Very upset*) She can't.

CLARE: It's a very difficult situation. I'm sorry. (*Gently*) Mr
  Mailer, there is a dress on the back of that door.

MR MAILER: I'm sorry. I –

CLARE: You live here with your girlfriend? Is that correct?

MR MAILER: Sometimes I think I can't take it any more. They
  want more and more of you, you see. There's only one of
  me, isn't there?

56

CLARE: I have to know what kind of home you could offer the child.
MR MAILER: I – (*Pause.*) Look. I love that boy. I love him. Marcia – (*Pause.*) Should you talk to Marcia?
CLARE: Perhaps eventually. But at this stage no. After all, your son doesn't know her, does he?
MR MAILER: I want him to.
(MAILER *comes in from the bedroom carrying a book.*)
MAILER: It's great, Dad. Thanks. It's really great. (*To* CLARE) It's *Myths and Legends of Ancient Greece.* It's amazing. It's great, Dad. (*Hugging him*) Thanks.

30. INT. STAIRS. DAY
Going down the stairs to the hall.
MAILER: He's nice, my dad, isn't he?
CLARE: Very nice.
MAILER: I think he's excellent. (*Pause.*) I'd like to live with him.
CLARE: Would you?
MAILER: Can I live with him?
CLARE: That depends.
MAILER: What does it depend on?
CLARE: On what the judge says.
MAILER: Don't you tell the judge what to say?
CLARE: (*Unnerved by him*) Er –
MAILER: Isn't that what you do?
CLARE: I don't –
MAILER: Don't you like my dad?
(*By now* MAILER *and* CLARE *have reached the hall. She stops and holds him by the shoulders.*)
CLARE: Look, Tony – where you live is a very serious business. Often we feel one thing one day and then another day we feel something different. My job is to try and help –
MAILER: I think you're a big shit.
CLARE: Tony –
MAILER: Big shit. Big shit. Big shit!!!
CLARE: Tony!!

(There's something frightening about the unfamiliarly harsh language and the violence with which he attacks her. As he screams the door upstairs opens and his father comes running down the stairs towards them.)

MR MAILER: Tony, what are you doing?

MAILER: I hate you!

MR MAILER: Tony!

(We see MR MAILER *clattering down the stairs as* MAILER *bites, kicks and screams at* CLARE.*)*

Tony . . .

MAILER: I hate you, I hate you, I hate you, stupid, stupid woman!!!

MR MAILER: Tony . . . *(Getting to the hall he pulls the boy off and embraces him.)* Please.

(The boy gets calmer.)

Please . . . *(To* CLARE*)* I'm sorry.

CLARE: Don't be. *(Pause.)* I really think you should talk to your wife, Mr Mailer.

MR MAILER: Yeah?

CLARE: There's divorce and divorce. And this is the worst kind.

31. INT. CLARE'S CAR. DAY

CLARE *and* MAILER *in the car on their way back from the flat.*

MAILER: Why are you taking me home? I don't want to go home.

CLARE: Why not?

MAILER: I don't like it there.

CLARE: Why don't you like it?

MAILER: I just don't. *(Pause.)* I don't want to live with my mother.

CLARE: You seemed happy enough when I called round.

MAILER: Oh, she's all right sometimes. I suppose. *(Pause.)* Is it because of the illegitimate baby, they're arguing?

CLARE: I beg your pardon?

MAILER: She had an illegitimate baby, didn't she?

CLARE: Did she?

MAILER: I thought everyone knew that.

CLARE: I certainly didn't know it.

MAILER: You're a probation officer, aren't you? I thought you found out about things like that.

CLARE: I'm not exactly a probation officer. (*Pause.*) Tell me about this baby . . .

MAILER: Ask her about it. (*Pause.*) It was called Alison. They got rid of it. (*Pause.*) Or I think maybe he killed it when he was rather drunk.

32. EXT. MAILER'S HOUSE. DAY

MAILER *gets out of the car.* CLARE *watches until the door is opened by* JOHN.

CLARE: I've brought Tony back.

33. INT. MAILER'S HOUSE. DAY

MAILER *enters and walks to* JOHN.

MAILER: Can Dad come to your wedding?

JOHN: I'll think about it. (*Pause.*) I will. Honest.

Day 43. Monday, 18 November

34. INT. SCHOOL. DAY

The class is waiting for MR POSNER. HUGHES, JACKSON *and* MAILER *are together coming into the desks but when they reach the point*:

JACKSON: Actually –

MAILER: Yes?

JACKSON: You don't mind if I sit with Hughes?

MAILER: Of course not.

(*But he does mind, desperately.*)

HUGHES: I've got an incredible hangover.

MAILER: Yeah?

HUGHES: Jackson and I went to this incredible address in Whetstone, didn't we, Jackson?

JACKSON: We did, yes.

HUGHES: Jackson's got a hangover too.

JACKSON: In fact yes.

59

MAILER: How's the new group getting on?

HUGHES: It's all under way.

JACKSON: We're called the Conqueroos.

MAILER: Oh. I wonder –

(But R. & B. is not his world. He decides not to say whatever it is he was going to say and relapses into silence as the other two talk. Enter MR POSNER.*)*

POSNER: *Bonjour, mes élèves.*

ALL: *Bonjour, Monsieur Posner.*

POSNER: *Tout va bien avec vous, mes petits?*

ALL: *Formidable, Monsieur Posner.*

POSNER: *Qu'est-ce qu'on va faire ce matin?*

ALL: *Du français, Monsieur Posner.*

POSNER: *On va parler, on va discuter, on va éprouver de telles passions linguistiques qu'on va voir nos visages rayonner . . .* Do you know what *rayonner* means, anyone?

(No answer.)

Et quoi? Vous ne vous sentez des petits français. Est-ce que vous vous sentez, comme des petits français aujourd'hui?

ALL: *Oui, Monsieur Posner.*

POSNER: Pos*nair*. Pos*nair*. Like zees . . .

(He takes a beret from his case and parades around in it. This goes down rather well with the lads.)

JACKSON: He's in one of his loony moods.

POSNER: Yes, Jackson, he is in one of his loony moods. 'Ee eez an' old idiot, no? *Est-ce que je suis un vieux idiot?*

ALL: *Oui, Monsieur Posner.*

POSNER: Pos*nair* . . .

(He loves all this, as do this class. A series of routines they have often been through together. But this time he decides to turn round and attack them. POSNER *takes out their exercise books and skims them across the room.)*

These exercises were bloody awful. Awful, awful, awful. Here is Bell. Bell is of the opinion that French is a syllabic language along the lines of early Minoan. Here is Bannerman who feels that it is not necessary to agree adjectives with nouns. Here are Carter, Dudley, Eversham

60

et al., all of whom have obviously raised collaboration to the status of an art, and beyond them countless misappropriations, acts of vandalism, pieces of wild half Franglais all the way down from Nugent to Yapping and finally Mailer. Well, Mailer, boy, you just haven't done it, have you? You just haven't done the work, it isn't there, I don't see any evidence of your having sat down with the text and looked at it; this looks as if a team of insects have been crawling across the page, I'm sorry, boy, it just won't do, will it?

MAILER: No, sir.

(*This hits* MAILER *harder than* POSNER *thought it would. The old-fashioned schoolmaster has got the better of the paternal bachelor.*)

POSNER: Quite upset me.

MAILER: I'm sorry, sir.

(*And* POSNER *sees how upset he is.*)

POSNER: Don't take on, boy. (*Goes to* MAILER.) Don't take on.

MAILER: I'm sorry. *I'm* sorry. I'm sorry.

Day 48. Saturday, 23 November

35. INT. MAILER'S HOUSE. DAY

John's wedding reception. A fair crowd. JOHN *making his speech.* MAILER *is at the edge of the group with* JACKSON. *The speech goes on across their dialogue –* '. . . to thank her for all the terrific food and my mum when she cooks really does . . .' *etc. Track across to find* MAILER *and* JACKSON *huddled on the floor together.*

JACKSON: Are you drunk?

MAILER: Pretty drunk.

JACKSON: The sausage rolls are good.

MAILER: And the pilaff. The pilaff is excellent.

(MRS MAILER *comes past.*)

MRS MAILER: Tony – where's the pilaff?

MAILER: I don't know, Mum.

MRS MAILER: And the rolls. Where have all the sausage rolls gone?

JACKSON: I haven't seen the rolls, Mrs Mailer.
  (*She goes on. Applause from the audience over by the happy couple* – '. . . John and Terry are really ideal and I know they're going to make a go of it because John always has a go at everything . . .' *Everyone having a good time.* MAILER *and* JACKSON *slide out the pilaff and the rolls from where they have concealed them.*)
  I prefer christenings to weddings.
MAILER: I do actually.
JACKSON: Funerals are quite good.
MAILER: I've never been to a funeral.
JACKSON: I had an aunt who died. The funeral was quite good. They had these prawn things.
  (*Both eating.*)
  I think she was an aunt anyway.
MAILER: Marriage is completely outdated actually. It's pointless. I don't know why they're bothering. It's legalized prostitution, that's all it is. This pilaff is really excellent.
  (*The speeches are still going on. All the self-congratulation and optimism of a wedding.* JACKSON *looks over his shoulder at the garden and freezes.*)
JACKSON: Mailer –
MAILER: What?
JACKSON: Your dad's in the garden.
MAILER: He can't be.
JACKSON: He is though.
MAILER: What's he doing?
JACKSON: Just standing.
MAILER: They wouldn't let him come. (*Finally he turns and sees his father.*) They said he couldn't come in fact. (*Getting up*) If she asks, don't say where I've gone.
JACKSON: All right.
MAILER: You really are my best friend actually.
JACKSON: And you're my . . . (*half joking*) second best . . .
MAILER: Who's your best then?'
JACKSON: Hughes.
MAILER: He's quite nice is Hughes. (*Taking all this more*

seriously than his friend) What's wrong with me then?

JACKSON: You're all right. But you go on about your problems a bit much.

MAILER: Oh. (*Pause.*) Oh.

JACKSON: I mean I know you have a lot of personal problems at the moment. But you are a bit of a pain most of the time. Hello, Nicky, how are you. Want a sausage roll – so what have you been up to then?

36. EXT. BACK GARDEN. DAY

We can hear singing and laughter coming from the house as MAILER *comes out to talk to his father.*

MR MAILER: Hullo, son.

MAILER: Hullo, Dad. I brought you a glass of wine.

MR MAILER: Thanks. Thanks very much. Cheers.

MAILER: Would you like a sausage roll?

MR MAILER: I would. Thank you very much.

MAILER: There's some pilaff too.

MR MAILER: No I don't think I'll bother with the pilaff. Thanks all the same.

(MAILER *takes it from under his coat and his dad gets a swig down him.*)

MAILER: Have you cut your drinking down to – manageable proportions?

MR MAILER: I try. (*Grin.*) Come out the side. They won't see us there.

(*And the two of them go round the side. The noise of the wedding going on in the background.*)

37. EXT. SIDE OF THE HOUSE. DAY

MAILER *and his dad.*

MAILER: What's that?

MR MAILER: One of the lorries. (*Grins.*) I'm driving it.

MAILER: I'd like to drive a lorry. (*Pause.*) You're bigger than anyone and if anyone gets in your way you just squash them.

MR MAILER: It's not quite like that. They have this thing called

63

the Highway Code.

MAILER: Can I have a go in it?

MR MAILER: I'm not supposed to be here really. I just come to see John.

MAILER: They wouldn't know. They're all drunk.

MR MAILER: You're probably right. Where shall we go? Shall we go to Southend?

MAILER: All right.

MR MAILER: I used to take you to Southend when you was little.

MAILER: Did you?

MR MAILER: I was brought up there. Shall we go to Southend and hide out? Shall we? Shall we never come back? Eh?

38. INT. MAILER'S HOUSE. DAY

MRS MAILER *is coming up to* JACKSON. *Speeches dragging on behind them.*

MRS MAILER: Where's Tony?

JACKSON: Er . . .

MRS MAILER: Where's he gone?

JACKSON: He went to see . . .

MRS MAILER: Who? Who did he go to see?

JACKSON: Mr Mailer was here.

(*Total collapse under adult interrogation. She has gone before he has a chance to modify his evidence.*)

I think he was only –

39. EXT. MAILER'S HOUSE. DAY

By the lorry.

MR MAILER: In you get then.

MAILER: Can I?

MR MAILER: Course. (*Holding him*) You're a bag of bones, you are, ain'cher?

(*Just as he lifts him in the air,* MRS MAILER *appears at the front door.*)

MRS MAILER: Put the boy down.

(*He lowers him.*)

MAILER: Mum –

MRS MAILER: Where were you taking him?

MR MAILER: For a ride, that's all. A ride.

MRS MAILER: I warned you about coming here.

MR MAILER: I wanted to –

MRS MAILER: You wanted to what?

MR MAILER: I wanted to see John. That was all.

MRS MAILER: Well, you've turned your back on your family now, haven't you? Now. For good and all.

MR MAILER: You're just hoping I'll crack, aren'cher? Well, let me tell you whatever that social worker says about me you don't stand a chance because the boy wants to be with me and when my lawyer's finished with you and your bloody nerves and the things you –

MRS MAILER: *How can you say those things in front of the boy, how can you? You say you love him, you don't love him, you love yourself and that stupid bitch who gives it away to anyone!*

MR MAILER: *Well, it's more than what you do, isn't it?*

MRS MAILER: *How can you say that . . .*

MR MAILER: *I don't have to listen to that, do I? I'm not going to listen to any of your rubbish ever again, you go and push a few Largactil or whatever it is you stuff down your throat and –*
(JOHN *has come out on to the front porch. The sight of him stops his father dead.*)
Congratulations, son.

JOHN: What are you doing here?

MR MAILER: Nothing. (*Pause.*) Nothing. (*Pause.*) I used to live here. That's all.

MAILER: Dad –
(*But his father has turned away and is clambering up into the lorry.*)
Dad!

MRS MAILER: Come here, Tony –

MAILER: *Dad!*
(*His father looks down from the cab.*)

MR MAILER: Go with her, son. I'll see you soon.

MRS MAILER: In Court you'll see him. And that'll – be for the last time.

MR MAILER: It'll be the last for you, you stupid bitch, you won't get a look in. Not ever.

(MAILER *goes after the lorry as it roars away. His mother, frightened, goes after him as he runs down the middle of the road.*)

MAILER: *Daddy, Daddy, Daddy!*

(MRS MAILER *grabs him but he struggles against her.*) *Get off me!*

MRS MAILER: He doesn't want you, lovey.

(*That stops him.*)

He wants that stupid woman. Not you.

MAILER: He wants me.

MRS MAILER: I want you, lovey.

MAILER: He wants me. He wants me as well. (*Pause.*) He does.

EPISODE THREE

Day 55. Saturday, 30 November 1985

1. INT. STAIRS. DAY
CLARE *coming up the stairs to Marcia's flat. Rings bell.* MARCIA *answers. A woman not unlike* MRS MAILER *in appearance but slightly younger and, as she hasn't had children, slightly less careworn, on the pleasant side of brassy.*
MARCIA: Oh. (*Pause.*) What is it?
CLARE: To see Mr Mailer.
MARCIA: What about?
CLARE: It's about his son.
MARCIA: You better come in.

2. INT. FLAT. DAY
In the sitting room. MARCIA *grins at* CLARE.
MARCIA: 'E's in the bath.
CLARE: That's OK.
MARCIA: She's here. Cup of tea? It's made.
CLARE: Thanks.
   (MARCIA *goes to kitchen, puts kettle on. Goes through to
   bathroom. Pause.*)
   Do you have children, Miss –
MARCIA: Mrs. (*Sharp*) No, I don't. (*A grin again.*) Don't have a
   husband neither. Not any more.
CLARE: Ah.
MARCIA: He didn't last long.
CLARE: I see.
MARCIA: I work for himself in there. At the firm. That was how
   we met.
CLARE: Yes.
MARCIA: You're a social worker aren'cher?
CLARE: Sort of.
MARCIA: You like to know these things, don't you?
CLARE: It helps.
MARCIA: I'd like a social worker myself. All of my own. Sugar?
CLARE: No, thanks.

MARCIA: He won't tell you anything so I better. Eh? (*Lighting a cigarette*) She hasn't been near him for five years. Not physically. Know what I mean?

CLARE: I think so.

MARCIA: I don't know what started it but little Tony was just a fluke apparently.

CLARE: Ah.

MARCIA: I'm not being too direct, am I?

CLARE: I always think it's good if people are direct.

MARCIA: Because I know you social workers like to know all the details. You know. Every detail.

CLARE: Yes. (*Pause.*) You do too, don't you?

MARCIA: What?

CLARE: Like to know all the details.

(MARCIA *laughs rather nervously.*)

MARCIA: I do yes. Yes, I do. (*Calling*) Malcolm!

(As MR MAILER *appears in a towel* MARCIA *turns back to* CLARE.)

You make me nervous, you do.

MR MAILER: Oh.

CLARE: I'm sorry to call now, Mr –

MR MAILER: Out.

CLARE: I just felt I had to –

MR MAILER: *Out!*

CLARE: I got the impression, Mr Mailer, that you cared about your son. That's the reason I'm here.

MR MAILER: I won't be a minute.

(*He goes.*)

MARCIA: Known the family long?

CLARE: I'm afraid not.

MARCIA: Couple a weeks?

CLARE: Sort of. (*Pause.*) Still. I always think you make your mind up about people quite quickly, don't you?

MARCIA: Oh – you terrify me.

3. INT. JACKSON'S HOUSE. DAY

MAILER *is sitting while* JACKSON, HUGHES *and* WANAMAKER
plus a boy called HIGGITT *play 'Hoochie Coochie Man' rather
shakily. There are two girls present. One called* SALLY *and the other
called* RUTH. *On the drum kit is painted the slogan 'The
Conqueroos'. When they've finished*:

SALLY: Fantastic.

RUTH: Absolutely fantastic.

SALLY: Fabulous.

RUTH: Really fabulous. Fantastic actually.

SALLY: Fantastic.

(*Pause.*)

MAILER: Very good I thought. Is that blues?

JACKSON: Yes.

RUTH: Is there a toilet here in fact?

JACKSON: Oh yes. Out on the right in the hall.

(*Enter* MR JACKSON.)

MR JACKSON: Utterly fantastic. Quite fabulous. Perhaps a little
loud.

MAILER: Hullo, Mr Jackson.

MR JACKSON: Hullo, Mailer. Is this beebop, rebop or dooop?

HUGHES: It's Rhythm 'n' Blues.

MR JACKSON: Ah yes. Ah yes.

RUTH: We were looking for the toilet.

MR JACKSON: Through there.

(*They pass him.*)

Who found the girls?

HUGHES: Higgitt did.

(*We see* HIGGITT. *Large and mournful and silent, as is the
way with drummers.*)

They were at this fantastic address in Palmers Green
apparently.

MR JACKSON: And what do you do, Mailer?

MAILER: I just watch. And sort of advise. Don't I, Jackson?

JACKSON: Sort of.

MR JACKSON: Look after your friend, won't you, Jimbo? Try
and keep the noise down to a deafening roar, my children.

69

I am in court tomorrow pleading yet another hopeless case.
(*He goes.*)

JACKSON: My God, I hate him.

MAILER: I quite like him actually.

JACKSON: Oh shut up, Mailer. I don't know what you're doing
here anyway.

MAILER: I'm advising.

JACKSON: You just hang around with us all the time and you
don't play anything, you just look and it's really getting me
down actually.

HUGHES: You don't even like Rhythm 'n' Blues.

MAILER: I do. I do like Rhythm 'n' Blues. I like John Lee
Hooker, I do.

HUGHES: You don't. You just pretend to like him.

MAILER: I do. I do like him. I like Bo Diddley too. And I like
the other one.

JACKSON: Which other one?

MAILER: The –
(*He's putting a brave face on it but can't keep it up forever.
His weakness, anyway, is the very reason they are going for
him.*)
Why are you all being horrid to me?
(*No answer. The girls enter.*)
Why? (*Determined not to show they've got to him, he goes to
the door.*) Actually I think Rhythm and Blues is stupid. I
think Bo Diddley and John Lee Hooker are completely
moronic and pathetic. And I think your group is absolutely
futile and out of tune actually and I wouldn't be in it if you
asked me. I like Beethoven actually if you want to know so
you can keep your stupid music and whatever they're
called, new wave or punkish or whatever. At least I have
some intelligence anyway.
(*He goes.*)

RUTH: Funnee.

SALLY: 'Oo's your friend?

70

4. EXT. STREET. DAY
Back with MAILER. *If he was going to cry there is no danger of it.*
He's a tough boy underneath and the incident has brought out the
anger in him, which perhaps helps him to cope. He runs off down
the road.

5. EXT. TUBE STATION. DAY
MAILER *crosses the footbridge over the track and stands for some*
time looking out across the London suburb. One train appears in the
distance. He dashes down the steps and into the booking office.
MAILER: Half to Holborn, please.
MAN: Return?
MAILER: No thanks. (*Pause.*) I'm not coming back.

6. INT. TUBE. DAY
MAILER *in the tube.*

7. INT. FLAT. DAY
MARCIA, MR MAILER *and* CLARE.
MR MAILER: What have you said in your report?
CLARE: You're not a very communicative family.
MARCIA: I think I'm extremely communicative.
CLARE: You don't talk to outsiders. And you don't talk to each
    other.
MARCIA: You do Marriage Guidance as well, do yer? On the
    side?
CLARE: I am simply –
MARCIA: No offence. (*Grin.*) I just thought you was getting a
    bit personal.
MR MAILER: Marcia –
MARCIA: Sorry, love. (*Pause.*) It's poor you. I'm sorry about
    you.
CLARE: Have you met Tony, Mrs Riley?
MARCIA: No. (*Pause.*) Not yet. (*Pause.*) But I love kids.
MR MAILER: It's true. She loves kids.
MARCIA: I love them.
CLARE: Yes. We're all supposed to love kids. Aren't we?

71

8. INT. HOLBORN STATION. DAY

At some point in the previous scene we should have seen MAILER *on the train, alone, perhaps overlapping the sound. The small boy in the adult world, looking nervously along rows of unfamiliar faces. A dreamlike journey for him. As his father breaks down we cut to* MAILER *on the tube jolting into Holborn station.* MAILER *changes to the Central line. He mooches along the platform. A girl of about his age, rather solemn-looking, is staring at the live rail. Her name is* KAREN.

KAREN: It's rather frightening, isn't it?

MAILER: What?

KAREN: The electric rail.

MAILER: Oh. (*Pause.*) Yes.

KAREN: I look at it for hours sometimes and think: 'Gosh. Suppose I fell on it.'

MAILER: Yes.

KAREN: I've just been to the National Geological Museum in South Kensington.

MAILER: Really?

KAREN: Yes. On my own.

MAILER: It's quite interesting, isn't it?

KAREN: Fairly, yes.

MAILER: I'm interested in fossils. (*Stiffly*) Although my main interest is mythology.

KAREN: Really? At the British Museum for two pounds you can eat as much as you like. You fill up your plate with salad. (*Whether it is the thought of the food or the girl,* MAILER *starts after her.*) I was practically sick last time.

MAILER: Really?

KAREN: Practically. (*Turns back to* MAILER). Would you like to come with me? It's near here. You can share my meal if you like.

MAILER: What sort of things do you like?

KAREN: Frankfurters I'm very fond of. And beetroot.

MAILER: I like beetroot.

(*And they disappear into the tunnel together.*)

9. INT. FLAT. DAY

MARCIA: Enjoy your job, do yer? Enjoy poking into other people's lives and being *right* all the time? It must be very nice to be *right* all the time, mustn't it? And never risking anything? I take it you're not married?

CLARE: No.

MARCIA: No children, have you?

CLARE: No.

MARCIA: I know just what you thought of me when you come in first. You thought 'common'. That's what you thought. I'm not bloody stupid, you know. You thought 'other woman' and you thought 'common'. I saw that on your face. You have little boxes you put people in, don'cher? And I'm in one marked 'common' and 'other woman'. Because marriage is so sacred to you, isn't it? I can see from the expression on your face how sacred it is. Well, you try it. Then you come back and tell me what's right and what isn't. You get some time in, Miss Social Worker, OK?

(*She goes.*)

MR MAILER: I'm sorry.

CLARE: Please don't apologize.

MR MAILER: I am. I'm sorry. She should never have said that.

CLARE: She needs you very much, doesn't she?

MR MAILER: Does she? I hadn't noticed. (*Pause.*) If you say so.

CLARE: Who was Alison?

MR MAILER: I don't know what you're talking about.

CLARE: No?

MR MAILER: No.

CLARE: You see I don't entirely believe all that is in Mrs Mailer's petition.

MR MAILER: Well, you're very perceptive then, aren'cher? For a social worker.

CLARE: But I'm not entirely sure that Tony would be happy with you.

MR MAILER: Do you usually discuss your clients to their faces?

CLARE: Oh no. I go in and ask personal questions and write

73

things in a little book and never ever get involved. So I
never get into trouble.
(MR MAILER *quite likes this* CLARE.)
MR MAILER: I tell you this. Whatever the ethics of it are. It's
quite nice to have someone to talk to.
CLARE: Who was Alison?

10. INT. BRITISH MUSEUM. DAY
KAREN *and* MAILER *in the Ancient Civilizations rooms.*
KAREN: What do your parents do? My father is a dentist.
MAILER: My father is quite a famous lawyer.
KAREN: Is he really famous?
MAILER: Quite famous. But you probably wouldn't have heard
of him.
KAREN: Is your mother just a housewife?
MAILER: My mother's dead.
KAREN: How awful.
MAILER: It was a merciful release in the end.
KAREN: Do you have brothers and sisters?
MAILER: Five. Three brothers and two sisters.
KAREN: How fantastic.
MAILER: It is quite. We live in a huge house with a huge
garden.
KAREN: I go to Lambourne Crescent School. Where do you go?
MAILER: Mountdale.
KAREN: Where is that?
MAILER: In Mountdale.
KAREN: Oh. (*Pause.*) Do you like music?
MAILER: I like classical music.
KAREN: I like classical music.
MAILER: That's why I don't go to parties.
KAREN: I don't go to parties either.
MAILER: They're completely stupid, aren't they?

11. INT. BRITISH MUSEUM. DAY
KAREN *and* MAILER *are both eating voraciously in the coffee room.*
MAILER: This herring is delicious.

74

KAREN: It is, isn't it? You can go up again and really stuff
    yourself.
    (*Long pause.*)
MAILER: Would you like to come to the cinema with me?
KAREN: I have to be home by six.
MAILER: Oh not now. Later.
KAREN: Yes. I would.
MAILER: There's a very good film at the Coronet.
KAREN: Which film is it?
MAILER: I don't know. But it's always a good film.
KAREN: You are funny.
    (*They have finished their respective meals.*)

12. INT. BRITISH MUSEUM. DAY
KAREN: I must get home.
MAILER: I must, my mother'll kill me.
KAREN: I thought your mother was dead.
MAILER: This is my stepmother. She's awful. She hits me and
    all that. She's really crazy.
KAREN: How awful.
MAILER: Not really. I'm a Stoic, you see.
KAREN: How do you mean?
MAILER: Cato the Elder was a Stoic. I think it was Cato the
    Elder. It might have been the Younger. But Stoics believed
    that whatever the hardships you had to endure them.
KAREN: They were Romans, were they?
MAILER: Yes, they were Romans. But you don't have to be
    Roman to be a Stoic. Could I have your phone number?
KAREN: Of course you can. Of course.

13. INT. MAILER'S HOUSE. EVENING
MAILER'S *coming in, with some stealth, by the kitchen door. His
mother is waiting for him.*
MRS MAILER: Where've you been?
MAILER: Out.
MRS MAILER: Out where?
MAILER: I went to town.

MRS MAILER: I was worried sick. Mrs Jackson said you'd gone somewhere.

MAILER: I went to the West End.

MRS MAILER: What did you want to go there for?

MAILER: I just —

MRS MAILER: Come on. Where did you really go? Were you with him? Were —
(*She is shaking him.*)

MAILER: Please don't. I —

MRS MAILER: Has he been round again? Has he? Has your father been round?

MAILER: He hasn't.

MRS MAILER: Has he?

MAILER: He hasn't. Honestly. He hasn't.

MRS MAILER: (*Stops herself.*) I'm sorry, Tony. (*Pause.*) John's found a place with Terry. I — (*Forlorn*) I just worry, that's all.

MAILER: You shouldn't worry. *I*'m perfectly all right.

MRS MAILER: Well, I'll make your tea.

MAILER: No thanks.
(*He goes towards the stairs.*)

MRS MAILER: You must have some tea.

MAILER: I'm not very hungry.

MRS MAILER: Oh, come on, Tony. Do — (*Suspicious*) Has he taken you out somewhere? Is that it?

MAILER: No, Mum.

MRS MAILER: I got you those sausages you like.

MAILER: Oh.

MRS MAILER: And some beetroot.

MAILER: Thanks —

MRS MAILER: I'll get it.
(*She stops at the door.*)

MAILER: Would they really let me decide?
(*He follows her to the sink.*)

MRS MAILER: Decide what?

MAILER: Who I lived with?

MRS MAILER: Well, I don't think you'd want to live with her,

76

would you?
(MAILER *stands looking at the dresser. A picture of his father and his mother.*)

Day 57. Monday, 2 December

14. INT. SCHOOL. DAY
The house meeting, held in one of the science classrooms, with steeply raked benches. Packed out. Behind, the demonstration bench. At the front are MR POSNER *and the house prefects; immediately to his left, standing,* PATTERSON, *who is the house captain.*

POSNER: Before Patterson addresses a house meeting I have a
    rather serious announcement to make. As you are all
    probably aware, Mr Duvalier keeps in the Biology
    laboratory a supply of mice, toads and fish for the purposes
    of dissection undertaken by A-level biology students. There
    has also recently been present in the laboratory a rabbit,
    although I must stress the rabbit is not, and has never
    been, there for experimental purposes. Last Wednesday
    night a group of boys entered the laboratory after dark and
    'liberated' the mice, toads and rabbit, leaving behind a
    message scrawled on the walls of the laboratory which
    warned Mr Duvalier in very crude and vulgar language of
    dire consequences should any harm befall the fish. I cannot
    tell you how seriously the headmaster and I view any kind
    of political extremism but when such activities are related
    to the animal kingdom, especially animals which are the
    property of the school, I must warn you that we will
    prosecute the culprits with the utmost vigour. As yet we
    have no names but I have to say now that the finger of
    suspicion points directly at a boy who is in this house. I
    think he knows who he is, and if he will come and see me
    after the house meeting things may go easier for him than
    he deserves. No one is more conscious than I of the basic
    rights of animals but I feel such issues should be *discussed*
    before resorting to burglary and vandalism.
PATTERSON: Well, I hope you all heard what Mr Posner said

and I must say stealing animals is a fairly low trick in my book. Now, as you all probably know, we are doing very badly on standards. By next Saturday the following will have completed an hour of fives or run twice round the crematorium: Samuelson, Runnymede, Zwingli, Mailer – (*We see* MAILER *in the body of the house. Sitting on the opposite side of a row to* JACKSON. *He has his hand up.*)

MAILER: Please, Patterson –

PATTERSON: Yes. Mailer?

MAILER: I'm excused the crematorium.

PATTERSON: Why are you excused the crematorium, Mailer?

MAILER: Because of my leg. I have a note.

PATTERSON: Well, you had better do fives, hadn't you?

MAILER: Can I do fives with my leg?

(*Titters.*)

PATTERSON: I suppose not. What can you do, Mailer?

JACKSON: He can hop.

(*More laughter.* POSNER *intervenes.*)

POSNER: Let us not spend the lunch hour discussing Mailer's ailments. He can do weekly fencing with Mr Horvatch.

MAILER: Oh, sir –

POSNER: House meeting over.

(*The boys get up. As they do we see* MAILER *and* JACKSON *remaining seated.*)

JACKSON: Fenc–ing . . . with Zwingli . . . and Samuelson . . .

MAILER: It's nothing to do with you, Jackson.

JACKSON: With all the top spasoids . . .

MAILER: It's nothing to do with you, Jackson. You're not a friend of mine any more.

(JACKSON *gets up, carrying a heavy briefcase with him.*)

JACKSON: Don't expect me to give you any more addresses.

MAILER: I couldn't care less about your stupid addresses. Me and my girlfriend go off on our own.

JACKSON: Girlfriend? Girlfriend? I'll believe that when I see it.

MAILER: You'll see it.

(*Boys are swarming round the bench at the front to collect the chits, assignments, etc.* POSNER *signals to* MAILER *over the*

78

throng. And MAILER, *putting his tongue out at his friend*
JACKSON, *or rather at his former friend, walks on down to*
POSNER. JACKSON *watches for a moment with all the baffled
fury of adolescence and then marches off.*)

Day 62. Saturday, 7 December

15. INT. SCHOOL. DAY
*The fencing club in the school gymnasium. There are some keen
fencers here, one or two, but the bulk of the class are weeds and wets
who do not fancy running round a cold field. Many people in
glasses.* MR HORVATCH, *the master, a handsome, mad Hungarian,
is facing a line of these creatures, brandishing a sabre. In masks and
jackets all.*

HORVATCH: Fenceeng eez not a sport for wimps and wets.
  Mailer –
  (MAILER *steps out, looking somewhat apprehensive.*)
  Hold your sabre in neutral so – hey – hey – Now defend
  yourself.
  (*He feints at the boy menacingly.* MAILER *steps back a pace,
  looking somewhat alarmed.*)
  You're a dead man. Mailer! Try again. Defend once more.
  (MR HORVATCH *by the way is an ex-Olympic champion. He
  weaves his sabre round* MAILER's *with trance-like skill.*)
  Hey ha hey ha hey ha ha . . . Zunk!!!!!
  (*He bashes him on the head with vigour.* MAILER *reels.*)
  Never mind. Samuelson, analyse the attack, please.
SAMUELSON: You hit him on the head, sir.
HORVATCH: Samuelson, I said *analyse.*
SAMUELSON: You hit him on the head . . . er . . . twice, sir.
HORVATCH: Haldemann.
  (HALDEMANN, *a large mournful boy, is the only one present
  who actually likes fencing.*)
HALDEMANN: You finally feinted in tierce, sir – to which he
  responded with a half-parry in quarte, whereupon you
  flèche-attacked his head, sir, which was undefended and
  the hit was undoubtedly good.

79

HORVATCH: Due to ze fact that he eez holdeenk heez sabre like a bloody cretin while I am steekeenk ze sword in every part of heez body my God you are lucky you do not live in ze eighteen century you are a bunch of cretins.
(*He yanks another boy out of the line and starts on him.* MAILER *returns to the line and stands next to* SAMUELSON. *Another one bites the dust.*)
Again!
(MAILER *turns to* SAMUELSON *as* HORVATCH *works his way down the line.*)
MAILER: Samuelson –
SAMUELSON: Yes?
MAILER: Would you like to be in the Christmas play?
SAMUELSON: I'm Jewish. I'm excused it.
MAILER: God. (*Pause.*) It was all your bloody fault he got stuck up there in the first place.
SAMUELSON: Nothing to do with me.
MAILER: God. I'm the Virgin Mary.
SAMUELSON: I'm sorry.
MAILER: My mother's a quarter Jewish actually.
SAMUELSON: It's not enough being a quarter Jewish. You've got to go the whole way.
MAILER: You're quite good fun really, aren't you, Samuelson?
(*No one is giving* HORVATCH *the fight he wants. He turns to* HALDEMANN.)
HORVATCH: Haldemann, come here and geeve me a veegorous attack!
(*And the two really go at each other. Quite exciting as good fencing can be.* MAILER *and* SAMUELSON *watch.*)
MAILER: Would you like to come to tea at my house?
SAMUELSON: Suddenly I'm popular.

16. INT. MAILER'S HOUSE. EVENING
MRS MAILER *and* CLARE *are seated at the table in the kitchen.*
MAILER *comes in. Dog tired. Walks straight through.*
MAILER: Hullo, Mum.
CLARE: Hello.

MRS MAILER: Aren't you going to say hullo to Miss Malleson?

MAILER: Hullo. What's for tea?

MRS MAILER: In a minute.

MAILER: Can Samuelson come to tea?

MRS MAILER: Who's Samuelson?

MAILER: He's my best friend.

MRS MAILER: Oh. I suppose so.

MAILER: Thanks.

> (MAILER *goes through to the hall. We see him unpack his briefcase and kick off his shoes where he is. Cut back to* MRS MAILER *and* CLARE.)

CLARE: He seems OK.

MRS MAILER: So long as he gets his meals on time. They'll let me keep him, won't they?

CLARE: All I feel is that if you could at least talk about it before it gets to the hearing.

MRS MAILER: I can't. I can't. I can't. I try to be . . . you know . . . I try to talk to him but I can't. He doesn't want me. Oh, he wants Tony.

> (*We see* MAILER *tiptoe from the hall. He listens in the hallway to all of this.*)

For five minutes he wants Tony but then that's enough. He doesn't really *want* him. He wants that stupid woman. I'm just showing him, that's all. I'm just showing him he can't get away with it. (*Suddenly very vulnerable*) I have tried, Miss Malleson. I have. He doesn't want me. And he wants Tony too. And Tony's all I've got, you see. You'll tell them that, won't you?

CLARE: Who was Alison, Mrs Mailer?

> (MRS MAILER *starts to cry.*)

MRS MAILER: Please. Please. Please.

CLARE: I'm sorry.

17. INT. MAILER'S HOUSE. EVENING

We see CLARE *come out into the hall.* MAILER *is sitting cross-legged over a book. He looks up.*

CLARE: Hullo.

MAILER: Hullo.

CLARE: Speaking to me?

MAILER: Yes.

CLARE: What are you reading?

MAILER: *Les Fleurs du Mal* by Baudelaire.

CLARE: Is it good?

MAILER: Very very good. Hard to understand but very good.

CLARE: Do you miss your dad?

MAILER: Yes.

CLARE: I'm sure. (*Going to him*) Look, maybe there's a way, eh? Maybe you won't have to choose. Maybe we can sort it all out. Don't you think?

MAILER: She's all right really is Mum. I mean basically she's OK. You know?

CLARE: Yes.

MAILER: She's not as barmy as she was.
(CLARE *sits on the floor. Like a lot of unassuming-looking people she has a real gift for getting on with people.*)

CLARE: When was she barmy?

MAILER: When I was small she was really, really barmy.

CLARE: Yes?

MAILER: Oh yes. (*Pause.*) She used to dress me in girl's clothes.

CLARE: Did she?

MAILER: Oh yes. It was quite embarrassing. (*Very matter of fact*) I was supposed to be a girl you see.

CLARE: Were you?

MAILER: So she had all these girl's clothes.

CLARE: Did she?

MAILER: In the end I said I'm not a girl. I'm a boy. I like being a boy. I want to be a boy. Stop it. So she stopped.

CLARE: This was . . .

MAILER: Ages ago. Ages and ages ago. I don't know why I just thought of it.
(CLARE *gets up.* MAILER *remains on the floor.*)

CLARE: Perhaps it was Baudelaire reminded you.

MAILER: Poetry is emotion recollected in tranquillity, you know.

82

CLARE: Is it?

MAILER: I'm not effeminate or anything. You don't think I'm effeminate, do you?

CLARE: No. I think you're big and butch and lovely.
(*She kisses him. As she goes out he follows her.*)

MAILER: (*Suddenly defendant*) I think I just want them to stop really. To stop arguing. You know? That's all I want.

CLARE: Well, I suppose we'll have to find out what they're arguing about, won't we?

18. INT./EXT. MAILER'S HOUSE. EVENING

CLARE *coming out of the house. As she walks down the street she is stopped by* MR MAILER *in his car.*

MR MAILER: (*Almost spy-like but subdued*) Hi!

CLARE: Oh hullo.

MR MAILER: I'm over thirty yards away from the house.

CLARE: Well, you're all right then, aren't you?

MR MAILER: And I'm sober.

CLARE: I can see that.

MR MAILER: Can we talk?

CLARE: Of course.

19. INT. MR MAILER'S CAR. EVENING

CLARE *and* MR MAILER.

MR MAILER: When John was three she got pregnant again. Anyway – it was a little girl. We called her Alison.

CLARE: Yes.

MR MAILER: I've never talked about this. Neither of us have parents who – I held her in my arms in the hospital, and all I could think was 'Why is she so quiet?' Then she was home and she was never right. I knew she wasn't right. And one night – she wasn't more than a few weeks old – I went into her room, her room was all decorated with monkeys and ducks and – (*Pause.*) She was standing over the cot. Her hands were over the covers. Like that. And she says, 'She's dead, Malcolm.' Like that. 'She's not breathing. She's dead.' And do you know that – all I could

83

think was 'She killed her. She . . .' I never said nothing. But that was my first thought. It was like she'd never been there. And we never talked about it. But it was always like she was between us. And we had Tony and we loved him, you know – but she was between us more and more and then she didn't . . . she couldn't . . . and Marcia . . . (*Pause.*) I haven't talked about this. To anyone . . .

CLARE: It's funny. I've seen an awful lot of divorce. And it always struck me as ugly or pointless or – (*Looking sideways at him*) Can you give me a lift? I haven't got the car.

MR MAILER: Sure.

(*As they pull away,* CLARE *turns to him.*)

20. INT. MAILER'S HOUSE. EVENING
Mailer's bedroom. He is trying on a very extreme-looking jacket. His mother comes round to the door.

MRS MAILER: Oh. Where did you get that?

MAILER: It's Samuelson's. What do you think?

MRS MAILER: Er . . .

MAILER: Do you think it looks good?

MRS MAILER: Oh lovely. (*Pause.*) Where did you say you were going?

MAILER: To the pictures.

MRS MAILER: Ah. Who with?

MAILER: Samuelson?

MRS MAILER: You're very keen on this Samuelson all of a sudden, aren't you?

MAILER: He's very intelligent.

MRS MAILER: Well, you're dressed up nicely anyway.

MAILER: He's very smart.

MRS MAILER: Saturday night. (*Pause.*) Everyone going out except me.

MAILER: I won't be late, Mum.

MRS MAILER: (*Stops herself*) Have a nice time.

21. INT. MR MAILER'S CAR. EVENING
MR MAILER: Look. Will you come over?
CLARE: To where?
MR MAILER: To the flat. I want to talk to you.
CLARE: Is Marcia there?
MR MAILER: I want her to be there.
  (*Pause.*)
CLARE: OK.

22. INT. MAILER'S HOUSE. EVENING
We see MRS MAILER *alone in the dining room. Cleaning again. Turns on the television. No comfort really. She sits alone. Staring out at the empty garden.*

23. EXT. CORONET CINEMA. EVENING
Over this we see MAILER *arrive at the Coronet and encounter* KAREN, *who is wearing a garment even more incongruous, should such a thing be possible, than* MAILER's. *He wonders whether to kiss her, decides not to and grimaces.*

24. EXT./INT. CORONET CINEMA. EVENING
MAILER *and* KAREN.
KAREN: What's the film?
MAILER: I'm not sure really.
KAREN: You are *funny*.
MAILER: It's been a terrible day.
KAREN: Has it?
MAILER: My sister fell off the roof.
KAREN: Oh no.
MAILER: She had to be rushed to hospital.
KAREN: I am sorry.
MAILER: And my stepmother was drunk.
  (*She looks at him. Is she starting to be a little unnerved by all of this?*)
KAREN: Your family does sound funny.
  (SAMUELSON *and* SHEILA *approach.*)
MAILER: I'll get the tickets.

85

25. EXT. STREET. EVENING
We see CLARE *and* MR MAILER *stop the car near Marcia's flat.*

26. INT. STAIRS. EVENING
CLARE *and* MR MAILER *go up the gloomy stairs. When they get to the door* MR MAILER *opens it and we see* MARCIA *sitting alone in the living room much as* MRS MAILER *had been, suddenly jerking into life at the sight of company. She's not too happy at the sight of* CLARE.

MARCIA: Oh.
MR MAILER: I thought –
MARCIA: What's she doing here?
CLARE: Mr Mailer wanted me here.

27. INT. CORONET CINEMA. EVENING
MAILER *at box office. He leans in.*

MAILER: (*Feeling extremely self-conscious in his gear*) Two halves, please.
WOMAN: This is a 15 film, love. You can't get halves for a 15 rating.
MAILER: Oh. Oh no.

28. INT. FLAT. EVENING
CLARE, MARCIA *and* MR MAILER. MARCIA *getting up and restlessly tidying the place.*

MARCIA: I don't understand you.
MR MAILER: Why don't you understand me?
MARCIA: I don't see what this is to do with her.
MR MAILER: Look.
MARCIA: I'm sorry. I'll go.
MR MAILER: But we've got to talk about it, love. We must talk about it.
MARCIA: I just don't understand why she's here.
MR MAILER: I just can't talk about it to you. That's all.
MARCIA: What's there to talk about? You're getting a divorce, aren't you?
CLARE: Tony –

86

MARCIA: Tony Tony Tony Tony. Please can we leave the kid out of it? Please. At the end of the day if you want to know I think kids look after themselves. I did. And I'm all right. Nobody helped me along. Shall we not talk about Tony for a moment . . . Shall we talk about me and you, Malcolm eh?

29. INT. CORONET CINEMA. EVENING

The object of all this concern is at the moment extremely worried. In a huddle with the others in the foyer.

MAILER: Oh, there's Samuelson.

KAREN: Where are the tickets then?

MAILER: I just . . . er . . .

> (*Plucking up his courage he goes back again in the hope they have forgotten.*)

Two tickets please. Grown-up ones.

WOMAN: You what?

MAILER: Two tickets.

WOMAN: You are over fifteen, I take it?

MAILER: Oh yes. Yes.

WOMAN: Weren't you the boy that was asking for two halves?

MAILER: Yes, I was.

WOMAN: Well, who was they for then?

MAILER: My little . . . brother and sister.

WOMAN: Well, you better tell them to go home then, hadn't you?

30. INT. MAILER'S HOUSE. EVENING

The kitchen. MRS MAILER *pours herself a drink and pushes the bar over.*

31. INT. FLAT. EVENING

CLARE, MARCIA *and* MR MAILER.

MR MAILER: All I mean, love – is – do you want him?

MARCIA: I still don't understand why she's here.

MR MAILER: Because –

MARCIA: I want what you want.

MR MAILER: I think maybe I'm being unfair to you. He's a boy. You wouldn't want him around. He's got his books and his mates and his . . . I don't expect you to understand what I feel for him or why I need him. He's my son, Marcia.

CLARE: I'll go.

MR MAILER: Please stay.

MARCIA: What do you want me to say, Malcolm? (*Pause.*) I want what you want. If you want him with us then that's fine. I told you. I love kids. If not. Then fine. Whatever you want I want.

CLARE: I really had better go. I just have to say this. Whatever you're doing, do it and don't use the child.

MARCIA: She bloody uses him all the time. Why do you think he's had to bring the action, you stupid bitch? Eh?

CLARE: I'm sorry. (*Getting up to go*) I'm sorry I came.
(*But* MARCIA *is now very on edge. Her hold on Mailer's dad is very precarious.*)

MARCIA: If you're talking about using, what she does is nobody's business. He works so bloody hard and all she does is take from him. Christ, I'm for being fair to the kid but how can you be when she . . .

CLARE: I'm sorry, Mrs Riley. This is really nothing to do with me. I should not have come. I'm sorry.
(*When she's gone* MARCIA *turns to* MR MAILER.)

MARCIA: (*Suddenly vulnerable*) It's make-your-mind-up time. Do you want me?

MR MAILER: I don't . . .

MARCIA: I don't want it to be me or the kid. I don't see why it should be like that. That's wrong, isn't it?

MR MAILER: I just –

MARCIA: Do you want *me*, that's all. And not her. Do you?

MR MAILER: Of course I want you.

32. INT. CORONET CINEMA. EVENING
Back at the Coronet the audience is going in. We see from the posters that the film is a horror film. SAMUELSON *and* MAILER *and the*

two girls file in and take their seats and the film, it appears, is in mid-flow. A big close-up of one of the space children with its mother. *We see* SAMUELSON *getting his arm round* SHEILA. MAILER *checking out where* SAMUELSON *has got to. He, very slowly, puts his arm round* KAREN. *She appears not to notice. On the screen a space child is frightening its mother.*

33. INT. MAILER'S HOUSE. NIGHT
MRS MAILER *is going upstairs to the bathroom. She sits on the edge of the bath. Staring into the mirror, wondering what she's missed. After a while she goes to the cupboard and starts sorting through the pill bottles, dead-eyed.*

34. INT. MAILER'S HOUSE. NIGHT
Mailer's mum in the bathroom. She pours a packet of pills into her palm. For a moment we think, or assume, she is going to go the way of wronged wives and swallow the lot but she does no such thing. In a sudden brutal movement she hurls the packet at the wall and snatching a glass from the shelf she does the same to it. Then gets to work on the bathroom, a sudden and shocking look at the woman suppressed by misery. Like her husband very, very violent.

35. INT. CORONET CINEMA. NIGHT
And on the screen at the Coronet appalling things are happening as well. Watched by SAMUELSON *and* MAILER *and company.* SAMUELSON *is doing rather well with* SHEILA. MAILER, *still checking on his progress, moves towards* KAREN, *swooping down his face on hers like some bird coming into land. Just as he gets there:*
KAREN: No.

36. INT. MAILER'S HOUSE. NIGHT
The implicit violence of their unsatisfactory encounter is made explicit in the next shot. MRS MAILER *finishes the bathroom and is having a go at more domestic icons. The bed and the photographs round the bed. All the symbols of the good housewife and mother are savaged. There's nothing comic about it though. Savage is the word. Desperate, breathing slow and hard, she wrecks photographs, rips*

89

curtains, smashes presents and mirrors with single-minded ferocity. She seems to be damaging herself as much as her home. Perhaps the two are no longer distinguishable, and yet, behind it all, the promise of release.

37. INT. FLAT. NIGHT

MARCIA *and* MR MAILER *in the flat.*

MARCIA: It's like that woman said. I'm sorry I shouted at her. You shouldn't confuse him, you know. Aren't I allowed to touch you now?

MR MAILER: Yes, I –

MARCIA: You do want me to stay?

MR MAILER: Yes. Yes. It's just Tony –

MARCIA: You know I love you.

MR MAILER: Yes.

MARCIA: Aren't you going to kiss me?

38. INT. MAILER'S HOUSE. NIGHT

MRS MAILER *pushes plates off shelves.*

39. INT. FLAT. NIGHT

MARCIA *is still very much the little girl.* MR MAILER *can't resist this. They kiss.*

MARCIA: One more time.

(*And another kiss. Intense, desperate sexuality about this.*)

40. INT. MAILER'S HOUSE. NIGHT

MRS MAILER *sits and drinks.*

41. EXT. CORONET CINEMA. NIGHT

SAMUELSON, MAILER *and the two girls.* SAMUELSON *and* SHEILA *are intertwined cosily but* MAILER *and* KAREN *stand somewhat apart from each other. They run and go. As they do so* MAILER *panics.*

MAILER: Good, wasn't it?

SAMUELSON: What?

MAILER: The film.

SAMUELSON: Oh, I didn't see the film.

(*And he winks as he goes.*)

KAREN: He's a funny boy.

MAILER: He is funny, isn't he?

(MAILER *and* KAREN *are using this word in different senses.*)

KAREN: Is he of the Chosen Race?

MAILER: He is Jewish, I think. (*Pause.*) I've been offered the part of the Virgin Mary.

KAREN: I'm going home now. Thank you for a delightful evening.

MAILER: Hang on. I'll walk you to . . . er . . .

KAREN: It's quite all right.

MAILER: No no. Let me. Let me.

42. INT. FLAT. NIGHT

MARCIA *and* MR MAILER *kissing in the flat.*

MARCIA: No stopping you, is there?

(*A sudden coldness which of course increases the passion of his next embrace.*)

Still confused?

MR MAILER: I will. I will talk to her . . . I will get it sorted.

MARCIA: You wait in the bedroom.

(*This last kiss is broken off. When he's gone she looks at herself in the mirror. She likes what she sees.*)

43. EXT. STREET. NIGHT

MAILER *is trailing desperately along behind* KAREN, *who is now making her displeasure at* MAILER's *weirdness – and, presumably his wild sexual excess – fairly clear.*

MAILER: There's a good film on next Saturday.

KAREN: Is there?

MAILER: I thought we might –

KAREN: I'm a bit busy next Saturday.

MAILER: Oh. (*Pause.*) How about – ?

KAREN: You're a bit funny. Do you know what I mean?

MAILER: Yes.

44. INT. MAILER'S HOUSE. NIGHT
MRS MAILER *in the kitchen drinking.*

45. EXT. STREET. NIGHT
MAILER *and* KAREN *at the bus stop. The bus is coming and she is getting herself ready for it. Rather a fussy little person she is.*
MAILER: How about the Saturday after that?
KAREN: Sorry, Tony. (*The brush off*) I've got to go now. Haven't you got to get home?
MAILER: I don't know. I don't know really.
KAREN: Bye bye . . .
    (*And she joins the queue off to the bus.* MAILER *shouts after her.*)
MAILER: *I'm not going home!!*

Intercut scenes 46 and 47 with MARCIA *and* MR MAILER *kissing and* MRS MAILER *tearing up photographs.*

46. INT. FLAT. NIGHT
MARCIA *and* MR MAILER. *The bedroom. She comes in. He's half undressed. She goes to the bed. They start to kiss and fondle again. Unstoppable.*

47. INT. MAILER'S HOUSE. NIGHT
And at home MRS MAILER *is sitting in the kitchen. She has taken a family photograph and is systematically shredding it. Everyone. She comes to Tony last and he too is ripped into little bits. When she's finished she leans her head into her hands and slumps over the table. Silence in the room. We see the wreckage around her, and the awful quiet of loneliness.*

48. EXT./INT. BUS STOP/BUS. NIGHT
We see MAILER *getting on to a bus at another bus stop. Alone in a corner seat looking out at the night streets. He is in unfamiliar territory. The conductor approaches.*
MAILER: It's in Acton I want.

49. EXT. STREET. NIGHT
We see MAILER *get off the bus. Walk down the street. He's looking at the street names. Doesn't quite know where he's going. Finally finds the road he wants. Almost at a run he heads off down it.*

50. INT. MAILER'S HOUSE. NIGHT
High shot of MRS MAILER *out of it. Drunk, slumped over the kitchen table. Hold it in total silence over the sounds of the empty house.*

51. INT. LANDING. NIGHT
MAILER *is at the door of the flat. The common door of the house is, as usual, open. He goes in and looks round the gloomy hall. Sees the name 'Riley'. Goes on up the stairs. Can't quite remember it all. Rings doorbell.*

52. INT. FLAT. NIGHT
The two in the bedroom.
MR MAILER: Oh Jesus . . .
MARCIA: Sssh.
   (*She wraps herself round him.*)

53. INT. LANDING. NIGHT
MAILER *ringing the bell again.*

54. INT. FLAT. NIGHT
MR MAILER: Ought we to answer it?
MARCIA: Why?
MR MAILER: Well . . . (*Grin.*) Might be someone interesting.
MARCIA: As opposed to me, eh?

55. INT. LANDING. NIGHT
MAILER *ringing the bell again.*

56. INT. FLAT. NIGHT
In the bedroom.
MARCIA: It's probably a Jehovah's Witness.

93

MR MAILER: You what?

MARCIA: They have special ways of ringing the bell.

MR MAILER: Yeah?

MARCIA: Very determined.

MR MAILER: They seem to have given up.
> (*The bell goes again. He gets up.*)

MARCIA: Now that definitely is a Jehovah's Witness.

MR MAILER: I'll go –
> (*He is at the door.*)

MARCIA: Don't go. Let them bloody wait.

MR MAILER: Can't you wait?
> (*He likes her need.*)

MARCIA: No.
> (*He stops at the door.*)
> Make love to me. Now.
> (*And he goes to her, kissing her. Very passionate. They fall across the bed, lost in each other. This should be direct and erotic. No trace of voyeurism in the way it is done.*)

57. EXT. FLAT. NIGHT

Outside flat. We see MAILER *hunched up against the wall, alone and miserable. Cold. He leans against the wall and tries to sleep.*

EPISODE FOUR

Day 63. Sunday, 8 December 1985

I. INT. MAILER'S HOUSE. DAY

The morning after the last scene of the last episode. The kitchen. We see MRS MAILER *stir, wake and then realize where she is. Not feeling too good, she gets up. Sees that it is light. Goes into the hall. Something's not right. What is it? Only then does she go upstairs to Mailer's room.* MRS MAILER *opens the door. The bed hasn't been slept in. She goes down to the telephone and picks it up.*

2. INT. FLAT. DAY

MARCIA *and* MR MAILER *in bed. The telephone goes. He goes into the living room, and picks it up.*

MR MAILER: You what?

> *(At the other end his wife is saying:* 'Where's Tony? Is he with you? He hasn't come home? Have you – ' *We see* MR MAILER *trying to absorb all this.)*
> Of course I haven't . . . I . . . Call the Law, I'm coming right over.

MARCIA: *(Following him in)* What's up?

MR MAILER: It's Tony. He's not come home.

MARCIA: Jesus . . .

MR MAILER: *(On telephone)* No, you call the police. I'm coming over. Now.

> *(*MR MAILER *puts down the telephone.)*

MARCIA: What's she been doing to him?

3. INT. MAILER'S HOUSE. DAY

MRS MAILER *sitting by the telephone in the bedroom.*

4. INT. LANDING. DAY

Outside on the landing. MAILER *is stirring into wakefulness. He yawns, gets up. As he does so, exhaustion hits him and he slides back down the wall. He is sitting there, staring ahead of him, when the door opens and his father comes out of the flat in a*

tearing hurry. Stops.
MR MAILER: What the – (*Pause.*) Tony.

5. INT. FLAT. DAY
MAILER, *his father and* MARCIA *in the sitting room.* MARCIA
and MAILER *are eyeing each other up with some caution.*
MAILER: Can I stay?
MARCIA: You what, love?
MAILER: Can I stay here?
    (MR MAILER *is on the telephone.* MARCIA *does not attempt to
    respond to this.*)
MR MAILER: Mary – he's here . . . no, I didn't . . . he . . .
    (*Holds out the telephone to* MAILER.) Talk to her, would you?
    (MAILER *goes to the telephone*)
MAILER: I wasn't trying to . . . I just went – Mum . . . I'm
    sorry . . . I'm sorry . . . I know you do, Mum . . . Mum
    . . . I just wanted to see him . . . I'm sorry, Mum, I just
    wanted to . . . of course I do . . . (*Near to tears*) Please,
    Mum, don't say that . . . don't say that, it isn't fair.
    (*Under the next exchange between* MARCIA *and* MR MAILER
    we hear MAILER *explaining that no he wasn't kidnapped, yes
    he is all right, yes he is sorry and all he wants to do is to stay.
    A few days that's all. The discussion becoming quite heated:*
    'Well, why not, Mum . . . I know I . . .')
MARCIA: He hasn't brought his things or anything . . .
MR MAILER: I'll go over there.
MARCIA: Malcolm, isn't this making things even messier?
MR MAILER: Look, leave me to do this, can't you? Can't you?
MARCIA: All I'm saying is it isn't going to make it easier to –
MR MAILER: To hand over my boy to her. No, it isn't, is it?
MARCIA: Look –
    (*But of course the physical presence of his son is already
    modifying his behaviour in a way she can't control. The boy is,
    after all, extremely tense and upset. His father grabs the
    telephone off him.*)
MR MAILER: I'm coming round now. OK? Now. We have to
    talk. OK?

MARCIA: Malcolm –
(*This is just what she doesn't want.*)
MR MAILER: Leave it out. Stay here, boy. I'll be right
   back.
MAILER: Dad –
   (*But his dad is going. And gone.*)
MARCIA: Well well. (*Pause.*) Nothing but trouble, aren'cher?
MAILER: I'm a bit tired actually.
   (*He goes to the sofa and lies down. Closes his eyes.* MARCIA
   watches him for quite a long time. Lights a cigarette.)

6. INT. MAILER'S HOUSE. DAY
MR MAILER *taking in the damage.*
MR MAILER: Having a party, were you?
MRS MAILER: I was amusing myself.
MR MAILER: I can see.
MRS MAILER: Well, I cook for you, I clean for you, I look after
   your children and –
MR MAILER: Please don't start that.
MRS MAILER: I'm sorry.
   (*The two of them go through into the kitchen diner.*)
   Well, all right then. Let him stay a couple of days.
MR MAILER: Mary –
MRS MAILER: He'll be back.
MR MAILER: Look – if you'll talk to me . . .
MRS MAILER: What? What if I'll talk?
MR MAILER: Look, I'll drop the hearing, OK? (*Pause.*) I mean,
   let's do it sensibly. Let's just try and sort it, shall we?
   (*But she isn't going to let him get away with that.*)
MRS MAILER: And let you walk off with her and see him
   whenever you choose. Oh no, thanks.
MR MAILER: Mary –
MRS MAILER: You take everything from me. You want to take
   everything. Well, you can't. You can't. You started it,
   Malcolm.
MR MAILER: Look, love.
MRS MAILER: Oh, 'love', is it? I'll get his things.

97

7. INT. FLAT. DAY

MARCIA *and* MAILER *in the flat.*

MARCIA: What brought you over then?

MAILER: I don't know really. (*Pause.*) I was a bit fed up.

MARCIA: I know the feeling.

MAILER: Are you going to marry my father?

MARCIA: I might.

MAILER: I just wanted to see him, you see.

MARCIA: Well, I expect he'll bring your toys over.
(*She gets up. Doesn't know what to say to him. He watches her closely.*)

MAILER: I don't have toys as such.

8. INT. MAILER'S HOUSE. DAY

MR MAILER: Why are you letting him stay?

MRS MAILER: I don't have much choice, do I? (*Pause.*) Perhaps I have been using him. I don't know.

MR MAILER: Shouldn't we talk about arrangements and –

MRS MAILER: Well, I was thinking. Last night. Thinking and drinking.

MR MAILER: What do you want?

MRS MAILER: I'll tell you. I want you back, I think. I want to talk. But not while you're with her. And if that's what you want, then fine. (*Suddenly, terrifyingly hard*) But if that's what you want, you'll have to fight for Tony every inch of the way. And I won't let you near him, I swear I won't. Because I won't forgive you.

MR MAILER: Mary –

MRS MAILER: I'm sorry, love. I think in some ways I've been at fault. There are things I should have done . . . I tell you I've thought. (*Touching* MR MAILER *on the arm*) But not while you're with her. You have to make up your mind. Which way you want it to be.
(*He can't cope with her now. She is over the stage of violent anger. He sits on the bed.*)

98

9. INT. FLAT. DAY
MARCIA *and* MAILER *in the flat.*
MARCIA: Your dad says you like acting.
MAILER: I do.
MARCIA: And what are you acting at the moment?
MAILER: The Virgin Mary.
  (*This completely stumps poor* MARCIA.)
MARCIA: Oh. (*Pause.*) Nice.
  (*The telephone goes.* MARCIA *picks it up.*)
  Hullo. He's out. Who's speaking please? (*Pause.*) Hang on
  a minute. (*Looks at* MAILER. *To* MAILER) It's your social
  worker.
  (MAILER *takes the telephone. Waits for* MARCIA *to move
  away.*)
MAILER: Dad's gone home.

Day 64. Monday, 9 December

10. INT. SCHOOL. DAY
The Big School stage. MR POSNER *is taking a rehearsal for the
nativity play.* MAILER *is standing centre stage, plus the shepherds.
In the front row of the auditorium, looking very professional, pencil
in mouth, is* SAMUELSON.)
POSNER: Mavroleon, you are a shepherd. You have been out in
  the hills of the Galilee. When you come into the stable you
  are freezing cold. And you are in *awe*. You are not walking
  into a shoe shop in Wimbledon, boy.
MAVROLEON: No sir.
  (POSNER *leaps up on to the stage with a theatrical flourish.*)
POSNER: And here in the crib, here is the Christ child. You do
  not walk up to him as if he were a particularly dull species
  of tropical fish. Do not peer. Gaze, Mavroleon. Gaze.
MAVROLEON: Yes, sir.
  (*He tries gazing into the crib. The effect is not impressive.*
  POSNER *watches closely.*)
POSNER: Gaze, Mavroleon. Not gawp. Gaze.
MAILER: Do you want me to pick Jesus up, sir?

99

POSNER: No, Mailer. I want you also to gaze. This is no ordinary baby. He is not an entry in some village fête. You turn to your husband – (*Glares wildly about him.*) Where is Joseph?

MAILER: I don't know, sir.

SAMUELSON: I think I saw Saltmarshe in the quad, sir.

POSNER: I have recast Joseph.

MAILER: Who's playing Joseph, sir?

POSNER: Your husband is to be played by someone with whom you feel comfortable, Mailer. Cast according to type –

MAILER: Who – ?

(*And from the back of the auditorium we see* JACKSON *coming in.*)

JACKSON: I'm sorry I'm late, sir.

POSNER: I hope you are sensible of the honour I do you, Jackson. Stand next to your wife, please.

(*As* JACKSON, *rather morosely, makes his way up on to the stage,* POSNER *goes down into the auditorium.*)

At this point, Samuelson, the lights should have a bluish tinge –

SAMUELSON: We can do you that, sir.

(*On stage* MAILER *and* JACKSON *are whispering furiously at each other.*)

MAILER: So when did you get involved then?

JACKSON: This morning. Just now.

MAILER: I thought you didn't like acting, Jackson.

JACKSON: I don't. He said I had to. I think acting's stupid.

MAILER: You think everything's stupid.

JACKSON: I think Samuelson's pretty stupid.

MAILER: You're stupid if it comes to that.

JACKSON: Shut up, Mailer.

MAILER: Shut up yourself.

JACKSON: I'll bash you in the –

(*Blissfully unaware of the friction between these two,* MR POSNER *leaps back up on to the stage and becomes directorial.*)

POSNER: Now, as the shepherds move forward, Mary and Joseph turn to each other with great pride, and this is the moment when Joseph, who is, after all, only a simple

Jewish carpenter, suddenly realizes the . . . achievement of his wife, and he turns to Mary, Jackson – (*Manoeuvring the two together*) And looks at Mary with love and awe and tenderness, you see, and Mary looks back at him with great affection, this is her husband, the person she has chosen to live with, and she too is deeply impressed and this gaze must be very meaningful and felt and expresses very positive things to the audience about the happiness of the couple who are, after all, the parents of Jesus. OK?
(*Pause.*)
MAILER: Yes, sir.

11. EXT. SCHOOL. EVENING
After school. Wandering away from the gates are crowds of boys. Among them SAMUELSON *and* MAILER.
MAILER: I think she was shy at first.
SAMUELSON: She looks shy.
MAILER: She was all over me.
SAMUELSON: The quiet ones are the most passionate in fact.
MAILER: Is that so?
SAMUELSON: It's often the case.
    (JACKSON *and* HUGHES *come up behind them.*)
JACKSON AND HUGHES: (*Together*) Here comes the Virgin Mar– eeee–
    (MAILER *rounds on them.*)
MAILER: Shut up, Jackson.
HUGHES: Shut up yourself.
    (*They pass on.*)
MAILER: Why is he like that? Why?
SAMUELSON: Don't worry about it. Don't you go his way?
MAILER: I'm staying with my dad.
SAMUELSON: Are you going to live with him?
MAILER: I thought I might. But his girlfriend's a bit . . . (*Taps the side of his head.*) You have to get your own tea.
SAMUELSON: Not good.
MAILER: I'll let them decide where I live. I'm fed up with it. I

101

can't take the responsibility. Do you know what I mean?
SAMUELSON: I hope they make the right decision.

12. INT. FLAT. EVENING
MAILER *coming into the flat.* MARCIA *and his father are there.*
They break away from each other as he comes in.
MR MAILER: Hullo there.
MAILER: Hullo.
MARCIA: Good day?
MAILER: Oh yes. (*Pause.*) What's for tea?
MARCIA: I don't think there is much, love . . .
MR MAILER: Never any tea here . . .
MARCIA: I thought we was going out tonight.
MR MAILER: He's got homework, Marcia.
MARCIA: Oh well, he's big enough to look after himself, isn't
   he?
MR MAILER: Give the boy a chance.

13. INT. MAILER'S HOUSE. EVENING
MRS MAILER *and* JOHN *in the kitchen. She sits at the table.*
JOHN: Look, it's all right, it really is. You mustn't let it get
   you.
   (*She doesn't react.*)
   I mean it's over. So, it's over. You're better off, honestly.
   Isn't it better, honestly?
   (*The doorbell goes.* MRS MAILER *goes to answer it.*)
   I'll get it.
   (*He goes to the door and opens it and there stands* CLARE.)
   (*Not at all pleased to see her*) Oh!
CLARE: I called your father, John, and it seems as if Tony is
   with him.
JOHN: So?
CLARE: I was a little concerned.
   (*Pause.*)
JOHN: You'd better come in.
CLARE: Thanks.

14. INT. FLAT. EVENING

MAILER *and* MARCIA *and his father.*

MR MAILER: Do you want to work in the bedroom, Tony?

MAILER: OK.

MR MAILER: I'll set a table up for you.

MAILER: Thanks.

MR MAILER: And Marcia'll get you something from the shop. Eh?

MARCIA: Course I will.

(*She has recovered herself now. But still finds it difficult.*)

MAILER: I don't like hamburgers.

MARCIA: Now how did you know I was going to get you hamburgers?

MAILER: People think all children like hamburgers. But I hate them.

MARCIA: Well. That's different.

MAILER: I don't like chips either.

MARCIA: Well.

(*He is beginning to get on her nerves again.*)
What do you like?

MAILER: Pasta. With tuna sauce.

MARCIA: Pasta it is then.

(*He has gone through to the bedroom.*)
Is he waited on hand and foot at home then?

MR MAILER: I'll have a word with him.

(*He goes through to the bedroom. Suddenly weary,* MARCIA *goes from the room.*)

15. INT. MAILER'S HOUSE. EVENING

MRS MAILER, JOHN *and* CLARE *in the sitting room.*

MRS MAILER: It isn't over. I don't accept that it's over. I just don't accept it.

JOHN: Mum, Tony –

MRS MAILER: You may not want him, John, but I do. I do still love him, John. And please would everyone stop telling me what's best. I know him. And I know when it comes to it he won't have the nerve.

CLARE: Mrs Mailer – your son –

MRS MAILER: *Please don't tell me about my son! I've cooked and cleaned for him for nearly fourteen years and he's quite tough if you want to know, OK? He may talk posh but he's a tough little bastard actually. I'm talking about me, OK?*

JOHN: I just don't understand, Mum, one minute – you're saying you can't stand the sight of him and the next you're . . .

MRS MAILER: There's a lot you don't understand. Isn't there? (*Pause.*)

JOHN: It's too bloody late, isn't it?

16. INT. FLAT. EVENING

MAILER *in the bedroom. Doing his homework. He stops. Gets up and goes to the door. We see through into the living room.* MARCIA *and his father.*

MARCIA: What's the matter with you?

MR MAILER: Nothing.

MARCIA: I got him what he wanted, didn't I?

MR MAILER: Look –

MARCIA: Did you talk to her?

MR MAILER: Yes.

MARCIA: And it is sorted?

MR MAILER: It . . .

MARCIA: I don't think you feel the same about me.

MR MAILER: I do.
   (*The little girl act again.*)
   I do, love.

MARCIA: I thought you'd do it. I mean I thought you meant it. And she –

MR MAILER: She what?

MARCIA: Well, she's got everything, hasn't she? She's got the house and the kids and everything. And you make a big noise but it's just noise. In the end you don't mean any of it.

MR MAILER: I do.
   (*He goes to her. But he's finding it difficult. And she of*

104

course senses the softening of his feelings to his wife.)

MARCIA: You've changed.

MR MAILER: I haven't.

MARCIA: Well, tell the lawyers you'll drop the application for a custody hearing. Say you want a reasonable settlement and she will go along with that. And stop putting me on trial in front of the boy, all right?

(MR MAILER *has seen* MAILER *at the door listening. He tries not to let* MARCIA *see.*)

It's you I want.

MR MAILER: I know.

(*She's in his arms. He's looking over her to his son.* MAILER *stares back at his father. Then, when he has seen enough, turns and goes back to his room.* MR MAILER *holds* MARCIA. *Helpless. They break.*)

OK?

MARCIA: All right.

(*But* MARCIA *can feel* MR MAILER *pulled towards the child.*) Tell you what. I'll go and get us a drink. Eh? (*With her cosy pub manner*) And you can have a nice chat to him. Eh?

MR MAILER: Fine.

17. INT. FLAT. EVENING

MAILER *in the bedroom. His father comes in.*

MR MAILER: OK?

MAILER: OK.

MR MAILER: You shouldn't spy on people, you know.

MAILER: Sorry.

MR MAILER: And you should watch your bloody manners. You know? Marcia . . .

MAILER: I'm sorry. (*Pause.*) I'll go home tomorrow.

MR MAILER: I didn't mean that, love. It's just –

MAILER: Well, she doesn't want me here, does she? She doesn't like me. I heard her. Mum said she wouldn't like me.

MR MAILER: She shouldn't have said that.

MAILER: Can I go home now?

MR MAILER: Give it till tomorrow.

MAILER: I don't like it here. I want to go home.

MR MAILER: *Well, why did you bloody come here then, eh?*

MAILER: I'm sorry. I better go home tomorrow and tell her.

MR MAILER: (*Near to tears*) Please, Tony . . .

MAILER: Do you like her?

MR MAILER: Who?

MAILER: That woman. Do you like her?

MR MAILER: Yes.

MAILER: And don't you like Mum at all?

MR MAILER: I –

(*Pause. The boy's directness getting to him.*)

In a way. In a way.

MAILER: I better get on with my homework.

MR MAILER: OK, then.

MAILER: I wish you still liked Mum.

MR MAILER: Perhaps I – (*Can't cope with this.*) I'll let you get on.

MAILER: Could you both come to the play?

MR MAILER: I . . .

MAILER: Because I'd like you both to come to that, you see. Whatever happens.

MR MAILER: Tony –

MAILER: You see, everybody else will have their parents there, you see.

MR MAILER: I –

MAILER: Could you come to that with Mum? Mum never comes to the school with you. Everyone else has his parents there. Both parents there. They'll think she's dead or something. Can you both come?

MR MAILER: I'll try.

MAILER: I'm not sure I want that woman to see it.

MR MAILER: *She's got a bloody name, you know!*

(*But* MAILER *doesn't crack. Just looks back at his dad. As his mother said, underneath the posh and shy exterior he's a tough little bastard. But perhaps all the more likeable for that.*)

I'll do what I can.

Day 65. Tuesday, 10 December

18. INT. SCHOOL. DAY
The stage of Big School. A nativity play rehearsal. MAILER *and*
JACKSON *are on stage while* SAMUELSON *and* MR POSNER
*clamber around the lighting rig. Also present are shepherds, Angel
Gabriel, etc.*
JACKSON: I'm going to ask to be excused Joseph.
MAILER: You won't be excused.
JACKSON: I'll say I won't act with someone who smells.
MAILER: Oh, don't be pathetic.
JACKSON: I'm glad you don't live near me any more.
MAILER: Oh, are you?
JACKSON: Yes, I am. It's really good not having you hang
   round.
MAILER: I must say it's quite nice not having to look at your
   stupid face every morning.
   (*These two quite clearly miss each other.*)
JACKSON: Hughes and I picked up a couple of scrubbers last
   Saturday.
MAILER: In fact Samuelson and I have regular girlfriends.
   (MR POSNER *descends the ladder on to the stage.*)
POSNER: Mary and Joseph, can you get into a position
   suggesting domestic bliss, and I want the Angel Gabriel,
   please. Schwaner, can I have the Angel Gabriel here
   too . . .
MAILER: Actually you will have to get used to me being around
   in fact.
JACKSON: Oh, will I?
MAILER: I'm living with my mother in fact. (*Pause.*) My
   parents are being reunited.
POSNER: The Angel Gabriel, Schwaner, is essentially a spirit of
   pure light, a presence, at once neutral and benign. You do
   not enter the room, you are simply there, as a healing
   influence.
SCHWANER: Yes, sir.
   (*He is a very small boy in a white robe with a pair of not*

totally convincing wings stuck on his shoulders.)
Can I flap the wings, sir?

POSNER: We have as yet no way of knowing that, Schwaner.
(MAILER *and* JACKSON *are still locked in combat.*)

JACKSON: Well, you'd better watch it when you come down the
street.

MAILER: And why had I better watch it?

JACKSON: Because if we see you . . .

MAILER: Who sees me?

JACKSON: In fact Hughes comes to my house quite often. For
tea. And if we see you . . .

MAILER: What?

JACKSON: We'll give you a going over.
(JACKSON'S *extreme gentility gives this threat a bizarre, comic
dimension.*)

MAILER: Oh, don't be stupid.

POSNER: *Mary and Joseph, could you arrange yourselves in a
position that suggests domestic bliss, please! (Bearing down on
them)* Do not comport yourselves like two horrible little
schoolboys giggling in a corner but in the manner of – oh,
Mavroleon. Mavroleon take the crook *away* from
Callendar; now, Schwaner, remember what I told you and,
go, the Angel Gabriel.
(*The Angel Gabriel, i.e.* SCHWANER, *waddles on without
much conviction.*)

SCHWANER: Er . . .

POSNER: Schwaner, you are about to announce the birth of
Jesus Christ. Could you please do it – with a little more
conviction. Otherwise the course of history may well be
changed.

SCHWANER: Yes, sir.

POSNER: Without the Annunciation, Schwaner, no Jesus. No
Jesus, no Roman Catholic Church; no Roman Catholic
Church, no Reformation; no Reformation, no Industrial
Revolution; no Industrial Revolution, no bourgeoisie;
no bourgeoisie, no First World War, no Second World
War, no post-war world, no Schwaner, Schwaner, no

you. Speak, boy.
(SCHWANER *scratches his wings.*)

19. EXT. SCHOOL. EVENING
Coming down the hill, MAILER *and* SAMUELSON.
SAMUELSON: How's your dad then?
MAILER: I'm staying with my mum, I think.
SAMUELSON: How's she?
MAILER: Oh, she's all right. Pleased I'm coming back, I expect.

20. INT. TUBE. EVENING
MAILER *on the train home.*

21. INT. MAILER'S HOUSE. EVENING
*We see his mother sitting at the table in the kitchen. She has before
her the drab correspondence of the opening stages of a divorce, not
yet the flood the thing can become, but none the less wretched for
that. Two opening gambits from solicitors and the first two letters
relating to the custody hearing. She pushes the letters away from her.
Feel her loneliness as she goes to the window to watch for her
younger son.*

22. EXT. STREET. EVENING
Outside Jackson's house, JACKSON *and* HUGHES *are fooling
around.* MAILER *slows, aware that this is now a danger area.*
JACKSON: I thought your dad was living at home, Mailer.
MAILER: He is.
JACKSON: Well, if he is, where's his van?
MAILER: Maybe he's not in yet.
JACKSON: My mum said he was gone for good.
MAILER: Well, it's nothing to do with you, is it, Jackson?
(*He starts boldly up the street.* JACKSON *stops him.*)
JACKSON: And my dad said your dad was always drunk too.
MAILER: Well, your dad's a stupid barrister, isn't he, with no
    intelligence.
JACKSON: Better than being a stupid lorry driver.
MAILER: He isn't a driver, stupid.

109

(He starts to walk past. JACKSON *grabs him.)*

JACKSON: Take that back about my father.

MAILER: Take that back about *my* father.

JACKSON: Why were you always coming round my house if
your mum and dad were so wonderful?

MAILER: Actually they're the best mum and dad in the world if
you want to know. They make yours look really stupid and
pathetic in fact. Let go of my jacket.

HUGHES: Are you afraid of fighting then, Mailer?

JACKSON: Yeah. Are you a girl, Mailer?

MAILER: Shut up.

JACKSON: Yeah. Mailer's a girl. He's a lovely beautiful girl with
all –

MAILER: *Shut up!*

HUGHES: Temper temper . . .

JACKSON: Just like his dad.

MAILER: What's that supposed to mean?

JACKSON: My mum says your dad knocks your –
(But before he has a chance to finish MAILER *has gone for
him. A real pitched battle.* HUGHES *joins in.)*

MAILER: *You shut up about them, you hear me? You shut up!*

HUGHES: Surrender . . .
(They've got him on the ground. We see MRS JACKSON *at the
window. She goes down, opens the front door; we see her
calling to her husband. He's coming out past her.* MRS
JACKSON *watches the rest of the scene from the front door.)*

MAILER: Never.

JACKSON: Surrender.

MAILER: Shut up . . .

JACKSON: Mailer's a girl. Mailer's a girl. Mailer's a –
*(At the door of Jackson's house is his father, striding out in rage
that is all the more frightening for not being actorish.)*

MR JACKSON: *What the hell is going on?*
(The two scramble off MAILER.*)*

JACKSON: Nothing, Dad –

MR JACKSON: *Nothing? Nothing? (At their side already.) Two of
you on one young – (Shakes his son. In a fury)* What is this,

child? What do you mean by it? What . . . is . . . this . . .

JACKSON: I'm sorry, Dad –

MR JACKSON: Are you all right, Mailer?

MAILER: Yes, Mr Jackson.

MR JACKSON: Run on home.

MAILER: Yes, Mr Jackson.

(MAILER *goes*.)

MR JACKSON: *I will not have bullying! I will not tolerate it, you hear me? It is despicable. I will not have the lad picked on like that!*

(*Pause. They look, as well they may, apologetic.*)

You know what that child must be going through. For God's sake. The pair of you. For God's sake.

JACKSON: I'm sorry.

MR JACKSON: I shall see you atone for this.

JACKSON: I didn't –

23. EXT. MAILER'S HOUSE. EVENING

His mother at the window looking for him. When he finally comes into view he is indeed a shocking sight – bloody nose, torn jacket, no sign of blubbing however. He comes up the path and his mum goes out to him, quite distraught. MAILER *almost fights her off.*

MRS MAILER: Tony. What the –

MAILER: It's quite all right, Mother. Quite all right.

MRS MAILER: Who done it to you, Tony?

MAILER: Just some boys. That's all.

(MRS MAILER *goes to the gate and looks down the street. We see* MR JACKSON *still doing his stuff. Pause. She follows her son into the house.*)

24. EXT. STREET. EVENING

JACKSON's *father seizes him by the ear and shakes him.*

MR JACKSON: And if, my boy, your philosophy of life is to be that the weaker and more unfortunate are to be punished . . . for the appalling crime of being miserable, just you remember that I am your father and I am a lot bigger than you and if I choose I can make you very very miserable

III

indeed. OK?

JACKSON: Yes.

(*His mother and father are standing united at the door. The perfect couple, impossible to get past them.*)

MRS JACKSON: It's so unfair, isn't it?

25. INT. MAILER'S HOUSE. EVENING

The bathroom. MRS MAILER *is cleaning him up with a great deal of care and attention.*

MAILER: It wasn't very nice round there . . .

MRS MAILER: No.

MAILER: She's rather peculiar.

MRS MAILER: She's a scheming little bitch.

MAILER: I didn't like her much. Mum . . .

(*She finishes putting a plaster over his forehead.*)

MRS MAILER: What?

MAILER: Someone at school said it takes ages to get divorced.

MRS MAILER: It does, I suppose.

MAILER: I mean, years sometimes.

MRS MAILER: Well, if you can't agree, it does.

MAILER: And can't you agree?

MRS MAILER: I think really, love, it's that I still want all of us to live together.

MAILER: And he doesn't?

MRS MAILER: He wants to live with that woman.

MAILER: But if I was living with you maybe he would want to live with you. Because of me. Because he might miss me.

(*The touching eccentric logic of this brings* MRS MAILER *close to tears.*)

MRS MAILER: He might.

MAILER: He said you wanted to divorce him anyway.

MRS MAILER: Did he?

MAILER: I think so. (*Pause.*) If you want him to live here why did you try and divorce him?

MRS MAILER: I –

(*For want of any easier answer she goes to the boy and puts her arms round him.* MRS MAILER *and* MAILER *sit together on the*

edge of the bath.)
I was angry.
MAILER: Because he was with that stupid fat woman?
MRS MAILER: Is she fat then?
MAILER: Huge.
MRS MAILER: I think I thought I could frighten him back.
MAILER: Are you still angry?
MRS MAILER: Not as angry as I was.
MAILER: Why don't you ask him to come back then? And stop
this stupid divorce thing?
MRS MAILER: I'll tell you, love.
(*Very serious. The conversation is just getting too much for*
MAILER *to cope with.*)
Sometimes you have to be very strong with people. And
seem to be very cruel. So that they can see what . . . what's
what. You know?
MAILER: I don't want you to, you see. I don't want . . .
MRS MAILER: Please . . . please.
MAILER: Can't you make it up, Mum? Can't you?
MRS MAILER: I can't explain it to you, lovey. You're too young.
There are some things I can't explain.
MAILER: Will you promise me one thing?
MRS MAILER: What's that?
MAILER: Well, will you both come to the play? Together.
(*Pause.*) Can I ring him and say you want to?
MRS MAILER: Tony –
MAILER: Can I? Can I do that now?
MRS MAILER: Well I . . . (*With some bitterness*) It's Christmas,
isn't it?
(*Pause. Almost resentment in the way she looks at* MAILER.
His passionate desire to bring them together is in one way an
expression of the prison in which she finds herself.)
Go on then. Call him.

26. INT. MAILER'S HOUSE. EVENING
MAILER *goes out of the bathroom through into the hallway and*
down to the telephone. We see his mother come out after him and

*look down. Then she goes to her bedroom. She sits on the bed, lies on
the bed. Stares at the telephone. Hears the bell click.*

27. INT. MAILER'S HOUSE. EVENING
MAILER *downstairs dialling the number. He gets through.*
MAILER: Dad? . . . Dad? . . .

28. INT. MAILER'S HOUSE. EVENING
*Upstairs in the bedroom his mother picks up the extension. Softly.
Listening.*

29. INT. FLAT. EVENING
MR MAILER. MARCIA *is behind him.*
MR MAILER: Hullo, boy.

30. INT. MAILER'S HOUSE. EVENING
MAILER *on the telephone.*
MAILER: It's about the Christmas play . . .

31. INT. MAILER'S HOUSE. EVENING
We see MRS MAILER *listening in.*

32. INT. MAILER'S HOUSE. EVENING
MAILER *on the telephone in the hall.*
MAILER: Mum wanted you to come with her.

33. INT. MAILER'S HOUSE. EVENING
We see MRS MAILER *in the bedroom.*

34. INT. FLAT. EVENING
MR MAILER *in the flat.* MARCIA *is coming up to the telephone.*
MARCIA: What does he want?

35. INT. MAILER'S HOUSE. EVENING
MAILER *on the telephone in the hall.*
MAILER: She said she'd see you there outside the gates at seven.

36. INT. MAILER'S HOUSE. EVENING
MRS MAILER *listening in the bedroom.*

114

37. INT. MAILER'S HOUSE. EVENING
MAILER *on the telephone in the hall.*

MAILER: Dad, she wants to be friends, I think. Honestly . . .
> (*We hear his father on the other end of the line:* 'OK.'
> MAILER *puts the telephone down. As soon as he does and
> before his dad has had a chance to replace the receiver* MRS
> MAILER *comes in on the extension.*)

38. INT. MAILER'S HOUSE. EVENING
The bedroom. MRS MAILER.

MRS MAILER: I want to talk, Malcolm. I'm prepared to talk but
we can't until you move back here. (*Soft*) Then, we can
talk. OK?
> (*We hear him on the line:* 'Mary – ')
Otherwise, you know what will happen, don't you? And
you won't see Tony. I won't let you. You wouldn't win any
case.
> (*She slams down the telephone. Cut to:*)

39. INT. FLAT. EVENING
MR MAILER *in the flat. Left holding the baby.* MARCIA *is beside
him.*

MARCIA: Was that her?

MR MAILER: It was.

MARCIA: What are they trying to do to you, love?

MR MAILER: What are you trying to do to me? Eh?

MARCIA: I –

MR MAILER: All any of you want is a piece of me. (*Going to
door*) That's all, isn't it? Eh?

MARCIA: Where are you going?

MR MAILER: Out.

Day 72. Tuesday, 17 December

40. INT. SCHOOL. DAY
*The afternoon of the school nativity play. The dress rehearsal.
Everyone on stage and looking fairly lost.*

HERITAGE: 'I this day throw off the Gods of Ashtaroth and Phem, the dark savage society of the Persians and of their so-called God, Rosarasta.'

POSNER: That was a shambles. A shambles. You, Heritage, are a magus, a wise man, an astrologer, and when you step forward to speak you should command the stage – (*Doing it for him*) 'For frankincense, the perfume of the wealthy, now hangs in wreaths about a humble stable, as a symbol that the order of the world is about to be reversed. Kings are commoners. Commoners are kings. All, all is utterly changed, and I this day throw off the Gods of Ashtaroth and Phem, the dark, savage society of the Persians and of their so-called God Zoroaster.'

HERITAGE: Yes, sir.

POSNER: I wrote these lines, Heritage, and I want them spoken properly.

MAILER: Who was Phem, sir?

POSNER: Good question, Mailer. An imaginary Phoenician deity. And from what little I know of the Phoenicians they are quite capable of inventing a God with a name as stupid as Phem. I made it up, boy. (*To the Wise Man*) This child, Heritage, by his presence, has healed the rift at the heart of the world, has remade the marriage of man and God – what's the next line, boy?

HERITAGE: What you just said, sir.

POSNER: Is it? Good God. From the top.

(HERITAGE *goes from the top. Not the greatest actor in the world.* MAILER *is standing alone.* JACKSON *comes up to him.*)

JACKSON: Mailer –

MAILER: What?

JACKSON: I wanted to . . .

MAILER: What? (*Pause.*) What?

41. INT. SCHOOL. DAY

MAILER *and* JACKSON *in biblical gear while all around them chaos continues.*

JACKSON: It's just that my dad . . .

116

MAILER: What about him?

JACKSON: Well, I . . . (*Pause.*) I mean I'm sorry and everything. About the other day.

MAILER: That's all right.

JACKSON: My dad said it must be awful.

MAILER: What must be awful?

JACKSON: For you.

MAILER: What though?

JACKSON: With your parents and everything.

MAILER: What about them?

JACKSON: Well . . . getting divorced and everything.

MAILER: Oh.

(*He is really not thinking about his parents at this point in time. In fact* MAILER's *probably not thinking much about* JACKSON *either. It is the play that concerns him.*)

I think they may not be getting divorced actually.

JACKSON: Oh.

MAILER: I thought they were at first. But now I'm not sure. Actually . . .

JACKSON: What?

MAILER: I think they're both a bit . . . (*Taps the side of his head.*) You know.

JACKSON: God, mine are. Worse than ever. My dad really whopped me the other day.

MAILER: I bet I could have beaten you if Hughes wasn't there.

JACKSON: Shake on it anyway.

MAILER: Shake.

(JACKSON *and* MAILER *shake hands solemnly.*)

JACKSON: I don't care if you do play girls in fact. You're much more amusing than Hughes.

MAILER: Am I?

JACKSON: Hughes is pathetic. We went to this address in Ealing. It was completely pathetic.

(*They are still shaking hands.* POSNER *bears down them.*)

POSNER: Mary and Joseph, this is not a Masons' meeting. Please listen to the Wise Man as he hams Mr Posner's impeccable prose. It is now nearly six o'clock. In a minute

117

we shall break for tea. All over London your mummies and
daddies who have paid good gold to send you to this
institution are on their way to see you celebrate the festival
of Christmas, the feast of love and family togetherness and
when they arrive they want to see something that makes all
that time and effort they have put into you seem
worthwhile, otherwise they may feel like sending you back
to the cleaners, OK?
MAILER: Yes, sir.
POSNER: OK.

42. INT. FLAT. EVENING
MARCIA *and* MR MAILER *in the flat.* MR MAILER *is dressing up.*
MARCIA *watching him.*
MARCIA: Going out then?
MR MAILER: I'm having dinner with a client.
MARCIA: Oh.
MR MAILER: Like the whistle?
MARCIA: Lovely.
(*She watches him. She has grown tenser with him since we first
encountered her.*)
We never seem to go out.
MR MAILER: We will.
MARCIA: How long have you been here now, Malcolm?
MR MAILER: I don't know. Don't know.
MARCIA: Seems ages.
MR MAILER: Not that long. (*Pause.*) A few months.
MARCIA: It's two and a half. But who's counting?
MR MAILER: I must go.
MARCIA: I'll come with you.
MR MAILER: I'm going to see Peters first then . . .
MARCIA: I'll come.

43. INT. FLAT. EVENING
Going down the gloomy stairs outside the flat.
MARCIA: Are you going off me, Malcolm?
MR MAILER: No.

118

MARCIA: Because . . .

MR MAILER: What?

MARCIA: The only thing I couldn't stand was if you lied to me. You know?

MR MAILER: We lied to her for long enough, didn't we?
(*There is that suppressed violence in him as he yanks open the door.*)

MARCIA: I'm just frightened.

MR MAILER: Of what?
(*They stand looking out at the street. Dim December day.*)

MARCIA: I think she's . . . you know what I think . . .

MR MAILER: You think she's using Tony.

MARCIA: Yes. Yes, I do.

MR MAILER: You think I've started something I can't finish.

MARCIA: I don't think you'd win any custody hearing, love.
(*Pause.*) They never give it to the wicked other woman, do they? They're all on the bloody wife's side, aren't they? Home and family. Isn't that it?

MR MAILER: Maybe it is.

MARCIA: Malcolm –
(*He starts off down the street. She runs after him. Stops him.*)
All of this divorce business. It is real, isn't it? I mean, you do mean it, don't you?

MR MAILER: I –

44. INT. MAILER'S HOUSE. EVENING

MRS MAILER *making up for the play. She has dressed with great care. Checks herself in the mirror. Stands back. Back to put a bit more face on. As she is doing so –* JOHN *and* TERRY *come from the door behind her.*

JOHN: You're looking smart then.

MRS MAILER: Thank you.

JOHN: We ought to go.
(*She can feel his anger at her urge for a reconciliation with his father. Goes to him.*)

MRS MAILER: There's a lot of things we should have talked about, John.

JOHN: I'm sure.

MRS MAILER: It isn't too late, is it?

JOHN: It's just Tony, Mum. I –

MRS MAILER: I tell you this, John. I didn't see any of this
clearly until I saw it was nothing to do with Tony. It was to
do with me and your father.

45. INT. FLAT. EVENING

MARCIA *and* MR MAILER. *He wants to get into the car and go.*
She wants to resolve the conversation satisfactorily. All the usual
preconditions for misery.

MARCIA: I just think I should be talked to about it, that's all.

MR MAILER: About what?

MARCIA: About what you've said to the lawyers. About what
she wants to do. About the custody hearing –

MR MAILER: There isn't going to be any custody hearing.

MARCIA: You what?

MR MAILER: Well, what's the point in fighting something she'd
win? And she says –

MARCIA: She says what?

MR MAILER: Oh, for God's sake, Marcia, you know what I
mean. The argument isn't about that any more, is it?

MARCIA: What is it about then?

MR MAILER: It's about me and you, isn't it?

MARCIA: And what about us?

MR MAILER: Well, can I face . . .

MARCIA: Face what?

MR MAILER: Living with . . . Tony just . . . It's bloody hard,
Marcia.

MARCIA: It's not exactly roses for me, love, is it?
(*But the ease with which she goes for the barmaid cliché reveals*
the extent of her defeat.)

MR MAILER: There are things about me and her I should
have . . .

MARCIA: What things?

MR MAILER: Well, it was like . . . (*Pause.*) After I told her
about us we were just trying to hurt each other. Any way

we could. And then – (*Pause.*) We should have told her
earlier, love.

MARCIA: Well, whose fault was that, eh?

MR MAILER: Mine. (*Pause.*) She'll fight it all the way, love. I
just can't take it. I've got to go back.

MARCIA: And how long do you think that'll bloody last?

MR MAILER: I don't know.

MARCIA: Are you going to see her now? Listen –

46. INT. CAR. EVENING

MRS MAILER *and* TERRY *and* JOHN *in their car on the way to the
play, not speaking. Then:*

MRS MAILER: John, you and your father have to talk.

JOHN: And what are we supposed to talk about?

MRS MAILER: I'm sorry. It's not too late. I don't think it's too
late. For either of you.

TERRY: Mrs Mailer –

MRS MAILER: I'm sorry, Terry, this is our family. (*Pause.*) I'm
not going to let it fall apart, John. I am not.
(JOHN, *sulky and silent.* MRS MAILER *rounds on him.*)
I've worked for you, and for Tony and for him, all my life,
all my working life. Some people might think that's
pathetic, that that's a pathetic thing to say. I don't think
so. I've brought up a home and a house and I'm very proud
of them and I'm not going to let them go. I'm not, d'you
hear me.

JOHN: If you don't feel anything for him, it's just hypocritical.
Isn't it?

47. EXT. STREET. EVENING

MARCIA *and* MR MAILER.

MARCIA: Look, you can't just go, Malcolm. I've a right to be
talked to. I've a –

MR MAILER: There's nothing to say, is there?

MARCIA: Where are you going?

MR MAILER: I'm going to the school.
(*She's holding him.*)

Get off . . .

MARCIA: You can't just go without –

MR MAILER: *I can do what I bloody well like, can't I?*

MARCIA: *Well, don't think you'll last two minutes with her even if she'll have you! All she bloody wants is the house and the children!*

MR MAILER: *Just shut up, can't you, just shut up! All any of you do is try and run circles round me! Just shut up!*
(*He struggles away from her.*)

MARCIA: *Malcolm –*
(MR MAILER *forces her back and gets into the car.*)
It's just like Rosie says. Always go back to wifey. Always back to the bloody kids, isn't it?

MR MAILER: I thought you liked kids.

MARCIA: Kids are a selfish heap of bastards. (*Near to tears*) Please don't go.

48. INT. SCHOOL. EVENING
POSNER *addressing the cast on the stage.*

POSNER: Quiet. Quiet. We have to make last-minute checks. Schwaner, Heritage, be quiet. Samuelson, get going on your sound checks.

49. INT. STAIRS. EVENING
MARCIA *climbing the stairs to her flat. She walks slowly. Going into herself.*

50. INT. SCHOOL. EVENING
The changing rooms at school. Or rather the classroom we saw in an earlier episode. MAILER *and* JACKSON *are getting into their costumes.* SAMUELSON *comes in looking harassed.*

MAILER: I'm not going to wear a bra. I'm not.

SAMUELSON: Herod's in real trouble.

MAILER: Where is he?

SAMUELSON: That's the trouble.

MAILER: Samuelson has addresses in fact, Jackson.

JACKSON: Really?

122

SAMUELSON: I've got one this Saturday, mainly Jews.
JACKSON: Girls?
SAMUELSON: We do have girls.
JACKSON: I'd love to come.
MAILER: The only thing is . . .
JACKSON: What?
MAILER: I don't think you could bring Hughes.
     (MR POSNER *enters, wild-eyed.*)
POSNER: The centurion's armour is warped. Warped.
     (*Exit* POSNER.)
JACKSON: That's OK. (*Putting on moustache*) You can't be
     friends with everyone, can you?

51. EXT. SCHOOL. EVENING
The gates of the school. MRS MAILER, JOHN *and* TERRY
approaching. MR MAILER *gets out of his car and we see the two
groups coincide. Very awkward.*
MR MAILER: Hullo there.
MRS MAILER: Shall we go in?
TERRY: Hullo, Mr Mailer.

52. INT. FLAT. EVENING
MARCIA *is sitting with a bottle of red wine on the table. Half of it
drunk. We can see from her eyes that she has been crying but she
isn't crying any more. She stares ahead of her with a curious
deadened expression.*

53. EXT. SCHOOL. EVENING
MR MAILER *and his wife go in front, a yard apart. The other
couple follows them.*
JOHN: Look at him. Just look at bloody Doomburden.
TERRY: Sssh. (*Pause.*) It's just for tonight.
JOHN: She'll take anything. Anything.

54. INT. SCHOOL. EVENING
Big School. MR POSNER *on the door as* MR *and* MRS MAILER
come in.

123

POSNER: Good evening, Mrs Mailer. Good evening, Mr Mailer.
MR MAILER: Good evening.
POSNER: Very nice to see you both. Happy Christmas.
MR MAILER: Happy Christmas.
> (*They make their way to their seats. Followed by* TERRY *and* JOHN.)
> They like to see it, don't they, eh?
MRS MAILER: See what?
MR MAILER: Couples.
MRS MAILER: Are we a couple?
MR MAILER: I don't know.
MRS JACKSON: Hello.

55. INT. FLAT. EVENING
MARCIA *in the flat. Really drunk. Stubbing out another cigarette. She looks old and ugly and lonely. She falls forward across the table, her hand going from the bottle. The bottle falls to the floor and the last of the wine spills like blood across her not-too-well-kept carpet. It is horribly quiet in the room.*

56. INT. SCHOOL. EVENING
The school hall.
MR MAILER: Look . . .
MRS MAILER: There's something I wanted to say –

57. INT. SCHOOL. EVENING
Behind the curtain the opening tableau is arranging itself with much giggling and messing about. SAMUELSON *is up in the lighting box.* MR POSNER *arrives. Gives the thumbs-up sign. Very showbiz. Then steps out in front of the curtain.*
POSNER: Good evening, ladies and gentlemen, welcome to the annual Christmas play and thank you all for coming. As the author may . . . (*Heard over the following dialogue:*) I apologize for any weakness and imperfections in the text. I have tried to tell the Bible story and give our fourth formers a history lesson at the same time. So if the dialogue seems somewhat dense at times reflect that as your children

speak they are at least engaged in what I hope is not a
completely unfamiliar process of learning something.
Thank you very much.

58. INT. SCHOOL. EVENING

MR *and* MRS MAILER, *in the audience, over* MR POSNER's *speech.*

MR MAILER: Look, it's all stupid. I want to come back.

MRS MAILER: Do you?

MR MAILER: If you'll have me. I mean I want to –
(*But up on stage,* POSNER *has finished his opening address and
the play has begun to applause. They break off to look up at
their son who, in a blue dress and hood, is pacing around the
stage with* JACKSON. JACKSON's *moustache is not of the best.
Somewhere in the audience are* MR *and* MRS JACKSON *who
are really not enjoying this, for reasons of family pride.*)

59. INT. SCHOOL. EVENING

MAILER *and* JACKSON *on the stage.*

MAILER: Oh, Joseph – if we had a great house perhaps we
could have children of our own.

JACKSON: We are too poor to have children. Children are a
curse, not a blessing upon a marriage.

MAILER: How so, husband?

JACKSON: For they interfere between the husband and the wife
and it is not good. No, I will never have children, wife.
And I advise you to do the same.

MAILER: Joseph – there are things I ought to impart to you.

JACKSON: What is that, wife? Is your mother coming round? I'll
throw that woman down the steepest hill in Nazareth, by
Moses I will.

MAILER: It's not that, Joseph. I think I am going to have a
baby.

JACKSON: A what?

MAILER: A baby, Joseph. Our baby.

JACKSON: It is not our baby, Mary. I would know if it was our
baby. I have read a little of what the Roman, Pliny, has
written and although he cites many a case of birth most

125

miraculously of the one body as Athena was born of Zeus, he does nowhere find the human animal capable of so breeding.

(*This example of* MR POSNER's *somewhat eccentric sense of humour gets a laugh.*)

MAILER: It is our baby.

JACKSON: It is not.

(*Enter* SCHWANER *as Angel Gabriel complete with wings. We see* SAMUELSON *in the lighting gallery. Desperately trying to get him to go into the follow spot.* SCHWANER *is mainly worried about his wings.*)

SCHWANER: Peace mortals, hear what I have to say.

JACKSON: By the God of the Israelites, who is this winged creature? Is he perchance a friend of yours, wife? For though our stories speak of such as the Theban sphinx whose riddles baffle even the wisest of men I –

MAILER: Joseph, I am a virgin.

SCHWANER: Silence, blasphemous fool.

JACKSON: Great heavens.

(SAMUELSON *has finally found the right angle.* JACKSON *drops to his knees unconvincingly. We see* MR JACKSON *cringe in the audience.*)

60. INT. SCHOOL. EVENING

MR *and* MRS MAILER *in the audience.*

MR MAILER: If you can –

MRS MAILER: If I can what?

MR MAILER: Isn't wanting to the main thing? Isn't that all really? I mean . . . if you really want to.

61. INT. SCHOOL. EVENING

On stage SCHWANER *is into his big speech.*

SCHWANER: God's son is conceived, fools. God's son is among you. God's son will be borne by this woman and the old world is surely dying, the law of the Scribes and of the Pharisees, the tales of the Styx and the imagined region above the clouds where Ganymede brings drinks to the

family of Jove and all his company. All, all is shattered.
God's son is conceived, fools. Hear me and tremble and
believe.

JACKSON: Great heavens!

MAILER: Now do you believe me, husband?

JACKSON: I crave pardon I ever doubted you, wife. I kneel to
you.

MAILER: No no, do not kneel, husband. I should kneel to you.

JACKSON: No. No. For wrong is wrong I have done you great
wrong by doubting you.

SCHWANER: You have indeed, Joseph.

(JACKSON *kneels*.)

62. INT. SCHOOL. EVENING
MR *and* MRS MAILER *in the audience*.

MRS MAILER: Well, I want to –

MR MAILER: Want to what?

MRS MAILER: Want to try.

MR MAILER: Well, I'm glad you do.

MRS MAILER: I suppose that's all we can say. For the moment.

MR MAILER: I suppose so.

63. INT. SCHOOL. EVENING
MAILER *stands before* JACKSON *on stage*.

JACKSON: Pardon me, wife. I am deeply wretched.

64. INT. SCHOOL. EVENING
In the audience of Big School. MR *and* MRS MAILER *staring ahead
of the stage. Dead-eyed. There is the feeling, however, that she is
seeing the same thing as* MARCIA. *Further down the line* JOHN *stirs
nervously and glances towards his parents.*

65. INT. SCHOOL. EVENING
On stage MAILER *out to audience with his hand on Joseph's head
as* JACKSON *kneels before him.*

MAILER: I feel the new God within me. I feel the power of light
which the old Greek Platinus spoke in his *Erineads*, the

hard and certain knowledge of what is true and cannot be denied, for the child that will come among *us* is to be as feared as his father and is as mighty and strange a presence to his earthly parents as any God or wonder of the world.

JACKSON: Amen.

(*From behind a row of angels appears for the first musical number. As the song starts:*)

66. INT. SCHOOL. EVENING
Finale of Christmas show.

> A child
> A child
> A child is going to be born
> Hold your horses
> Catch your breath
> This little child can conquer death
> A child
> A child
> A child is on his way.
>
> He's a winner he's the great beginner
> He's the start of something special and new
> He's no sinner he's born in a
> Stable and I'll tell you something new
>
> Look out the wicked look out the bad
> Look out the old old ways
> Someone's comin' along in the world,
> Someone's just rung a gong in the world
> And you're all gonna sing his praise
>
> ('A child, etc.' reprise)
>
> He's the bright one, he's the right one
> He's better than summer's day
> He'll tell his Mamma and he'll tell his Papa –
> This child is gonna show them the way

Look out Mamma, look out Papa
Look out sinners and saints
Someone's a-comin' a little boy's a-drummin'
And he's gonna be a regular prince so

(*Reprise chorus 'A child, etc.' plus not too good dance routine
choreographed by* POSNER. *Halfway through freeze on the two
parents staring ahead of them and, over their faces, superimpose
the final dialogue.*)

MR MAILER: When was that taken?

MRS MAILER: Well it must be ten years, twelve years ago at the
Christmas concert.

MR MAILER: I remember. What do we do with it?

MRS MAILER: Does he want it?

MR MAILER: He doesn't want any of them. (*Pause.*) I quite like
it.

MRS MAILER: You keep it then.

MR MAILER: I'd like this graduation thing.

MRS MAILER: He's done very well, Malcolm. Very well. But
you get what you pay for, don't you?

MR MAILER: How do you mean?

MRS MAILER: With education you get what you pay for.

MR MAILER: It all depends, I suppose. I'd better go. The
neighbours will think I've moved back in.

MRS MAILER: Doesn't Tony want *any* of this stuff?

MR MAILER: Well, there's no point in being sentimental, is
there?

MRS MAILER: No, there's no point in being sentimental.